Chapter 1

The Phoenix

The year is 2082, earth has become dense in population and its resources are being strangled because of this. New sources need to be found to feed the ever growing need of earth's ever growing thirst for technology. So the adventure begins.

Space has become the target for many opportunists, though they are limited by time and space in their ventures, as you will see, the Phoenix is not.

The Phoenix is a modest ship with room for a compliment of ten.

The bridge is small but functional with a co-pilot to assist.

Upon leaving the comfort of earth and the familiar, the crew of the Phoenix venture towards an unknown planet with a glowing red sun known as XALON52. XALON is some one thousand two hundred and fifty light years from earth. Very little is known of the planet except that it has oxygen and water. The needed Elements to sustain earths technology is also assumed to be there. Without these, the earth is destined to go back to the stone age of technology. Even electricity will cease to exist.

The intent is to survey the mineral content to hopefully find a new mining venture for earth.

The first officer and Copilot is capable and very familiar with the way the captain sees things, she should be since Kathy is his wife. Sometimes she wants to control the ship.

The science officer, Russell, twenty six years old, is at times moody and confrontational but adept in his field. Brown hair and blue eyes he stands at six foot two with an athletic build.

Rebecca, thirty years old, is the security officer. She comes from a black ops contractor for the highest bidding government or individual on earth. Her reputation is second to none. Standing at six foot one, blonde hair, and well-endowed woman can out run and out fight most men and species.

Lizzy, nineteen years old, is the youngest navigator the captain has ever seen. She knows the stars as if they were her home town neighborhood. I thought only God new all of them by name, in Lizzy's case he has competition.

They are traveling through space through a manipulated warping of space; this allows the Phoenix to fold space in a way to take short cuts over and over again. The warp drive is a personal design based on the light drives of the day. The captain has always seen things in a different way, opportunities instead of obstacles. This warp drive was simply a childhood fantasy that has worked its way into practical application.

As for the captain, his name is Michael, in his fifties with salt and pepper hair, six two and just at two hundred pounds on a good day. Kathy his lovely wife of thirty years is a brunette with beautiful blue eyes. Tall for a woman at five ten, she is curvaceous and a true compliment for his obnoxious disposition. He won't tell her, but she is the smart one.

The ship, the Phoenix, is a small and agile frigate with a compliment of weapons for defense and metaphasic shields. Her armor is a personal design which allows concussion, energy and projectile weapons to bounce off her like ping pong balls to a wall. She isn't impenetrable by no means, she has a soft underbelly but with careful piloting she can withstand the toughest of dog fights.

They have just left Earth's orbit and are on their way to the first destination, Space Station Alpha 1. The oldest of Earths space stations and the largest. There they plan on acquiring iridium and helium for journey to their destination. These elements are crucial for survival on the journey. From there they will start the first of many warps to get to the destination of XALON52.

Chapter 2

The Orion Syndicate

Los Angeles, Earth 2082

Orion World Headquarters

Paul Orion sits at his large desk in the one hundred twenty story high rise overlooking the skyline of Los Angeles. Orion, got his money the old fashion way, he inherited it. He now leads the largest geological company in the known sector. He has made his trillions in mining asteroids and has staked questionable claims on planets within the solar system. He has a hand in many other enterprises, many of which are deceitful and questionable as to their monetary gains.

The Orion Tower as this building egotistically is called, is the tallest building in North America. Equipped with a personal transport drone for Mr. Wonderful to jet about anywhere he wishes.

Today, is unlike other days, his greed is heightened by the fact that the Phoenix has launched to reach new geological discoveries in places his syndicate cannot reach. The warp drive schematics are what dreams are made of for this ambitious and ruthless man.

He summons his old friend and second in command of his empire Stan Whittaker. Stan enters Orion's luxurious office.

Orion: "Sit down Stan, we have a situation we need rectified right away."

Stan: "The Phoenix?"

Orion: "Yes! It launched today and is on its way to Space Station Alpha 1. We need to get there ahead of it and negotiate the purchase of the Warp Drive Schematics."

Stan: "We have tried talking with Mike before and he, well, he is stubborn. He simply doesn't need money. What can we offer him?"

Orion: Raising his voice, "OFFER HIM ANYTHING! ANY AMOUNT! I want that technology no matter what!"

Stan: "I see, if he doesn't want payment, then..."

Orion: "Take it from him!"

Stan: "Understood."

At that Stan calmly stood up from his chair and proceeded to exit the office before first turning around and addressing Orion one last time, "I won't let you down Paul."

Orion: "I know you won't."

Chapter 3

Space Station Alpha 1

The Phoenix floated through space effortlessly. Lizzy was at her station calculating the trajectory from one sling shot to another to get the crew safely to their destination. Rebecca, was going through her inventory of weapons, a host of fire arms, ranging from hand held focused ionized pistols to sharp shooter long range metaphasic projectile rifles. I seem to see the gleam in her eye when it came to hand held knives, she was an expert in close quarter fighting, and knives suited her style best.

Russell, was in his corner trying to drum up any additional information he could on Xalon52. The mystery of the planet intrigued him. He kind of looked at himself as an explorer, a discoverer and a savior all rolled into one.

The captain was at the helm with Kathy as they received the navigation plans from Lizzy and adjusted their trajectory accordingly.

This old but functional space station they are heading towards has a permanent crew and occupancy of ten thousand four hundred and fifty at last census. It is vast with modules connected with transport bridges from one to another. Within each living and occupancy module artificial gravity is set up, although outside those modules gravity is turned off for the free flow of transport modules. Each module can carry twenty five individuals with a controller at the helm.

In Alpha One, it is essentially a city with all the amenities and the challenges any city would have. The police force is made up of ex-military units from the interplanetary armed forces (IAF). Like any other city a mayor or in this case a Commanding Governor oversees the operation and oversees all its police and commerce capabilities. The CG in this station is Rukkus Mastadon, most just call him Rukkus. He leads with a heavy hand under strict military code. His subordinates are required to salute him as if he was a high ranking general. Rukkus, though has never served in the military and whispers about him being up for bid is not entirely untrue. Rukkus, can be bought and the station is rumored of being a way station for the black market and drug trade.

Michael: “Prepare for docking procedures.”

Kathy: “Aye Aye!”

As the Phoenix approaches the docking bay, it swings its bow around exposing the starboard hatch door. With great care Michael adjusts the rotation and positioning thrusters to gingerly hit the docking cushions on the bay. Clamps immediately come down and lock the ship in place; air can be heard filling the cavities vacuum. With a green hatch light located just above the exit, it is safe for them to open the door to the space station.

Michael looking at Kathy, "Summon the crew to meet me in the strategy room."

Kathy: "You got it." She reached above her and flipped a switch that triggered a flashing light on the com panels of each of the crew, "Attention, all crew members assemble in the strategy room for further directions. Out!"

Michael and Kathy secured the helm through a series of flipping switches and turning of dials before they got up to head toward the strategy room. The walk lead them down and then left as the ducked through hatches about five and a half feet tall. These hatches were designed to secure each section of the ship in case of a hull breach. The strategy room was about eighty feet down the left corridor, upon entering the octagonal room they were greeted by the entire crew, Rebecca, Russell, Lizzy, Zeeke and Longbow.

Zeeke, was a wizard at keeping the Phoenix running at optimal performance. Zeeke has been around awhile and knows the captain from grade school; in fact Zeeke helped develop the warp drive and fine-tuned the beautiful frigate they will be calling home for a while. In his fities also, balding from the front his brown eyes and pot belly give the impression that this six foot framed man has had one too many beers on his days off.

Longbow, as he likes to be called, is Rebecca's right hand man. Platonic is their relationship although many men would wish they could catch the statuesque blonde beauty's attention. Longbow is African descent although born and raised in Birmingham England, a strong British accent goes with his strong persona.

Upon Michael and Kathy entering the room, all stand at attention.

Mike, "At ease." motioning to them to have a seat.

They all sat down at the long table in high back black chairs waiting for the download. In front of each of the crew was a recessed screen embedded in the table, touch sensitive and at the touch of a button each could share their information with any and all seated at the table.

Michael, "I need each of you to be swift about your assignments while we are here. Rebecca, I need you to secure enough iridium for our mission. You will be going to module six, compartment three in the storage facility, there you will meet the dock master Kevin Runtundra, he knows what we need and I have negotiated payment as soon as he delivers the goods.

"Longbow, I need you to stay here as these materials arrive and guard the delivery and secure the ship, there are people wanting to sabotage this venture, and as you all know the CG at this outpost has been purchased by Paul Orion who would stop at nothing to get his hands on this ship.

“Zeeke, you will go to engineering, module two, compartment eighty one and meet Teufel Hunden, he will arrange the delivery of the Helium we need. He knows the amount and he too is aware of payment upon delivery of the helium.

“Russell and Lizzy you have enough here to keep you busy, Lizzy, we have four warp jumps in order to get to our destination, you need to get us there within those four jumps.

“Kathy and I will be heading to module one, forward deck. I see an old friend I need to meet before we set sail for Xalon52. Does everyone understand their assignments? Any questions?”

Longbow in a thick British accent, “Aye Captain! The ship will be as secure as if I was in my mums bosom.”

Rebecca: “Should I expect any surprises on this station?”

Kathy: “I would be surprised if Rukkus would try anything within this jurisdiction, I wouldn’t be surprised if, after departure, we get a surprise or two.”

Rebecca gives Longbow a long stare.

Michael, “Are we good?”

All of them in unison “Aye!”

At that they all exited the room all heading directly to their assignments.

Kathy, “Who is this old friend we need to see?”

Michael, “Pankaj Patel”

Kathy, “It’s been a long time, how’s he doing?”

Michael, “Making money from a distance. That’s how he likes it. Rich and behind the scenes.”

Kathy, “Why Pankaj?”

Michael, “He is familiar with Paul Orion, he knows what I need to know about what Orion has in store for us and how we can defeat him.”

Michael and Kathy make their way down a long corridor to a small hanger where transports are waiting for passengers. A rather large, what looks like a storage container with windows begins the assent to the landing platform.

Michael smiled “Here comes our ride.”

The transport lands gently down in front of them, two large doors open and twenty or so passengers exit carrying a variety of bags and luggage. Michael leads the way with Kathy close behind and enters the rather plain compartment with seating made for a very short journey. Close behind several more passengers gain entry, one of whom is Stan Whittaker. Stan hides behind the crowd while he eyes Michael and Kathy seated towards the front. Stan takes a seat in the rear. The crafts doors close hydraulically and then the craft ascends to the vacuum of space heading towards module one.

Stan Whittaker looks at his watch which is linked to his communicator, he begins to type *Made contact, in transporter heading to module one, will continue surveillance before the meet.* He looked up to make sure nobody was watching him, slouching in his chair to reduce his visibility.

The fifteen minutes without gravity would make many sick to their stomach. Michael and Kathy were used to the transition from gravity to weightlessness. The passengers seem to be relatively comfortable continuing their conversations without interruption. Fifteen minutes of weightlessness is a lifetime in perception, imagine free falling for that amount of time, nonetheless, the ship enters Module One and normal gravity is restored. Upon landing the captain of the little vessel issues exit instructions and then the doors open. Michael and Kathy get up and through his peripheral vision he sees Stan hiding in his seat. Michael continues as if he did not notice him and both he and Kathy exit the shuttle. They enter a crowded Aero Lift, an elevator designed to go not only vertically but horizontally. They touch the pad located to the right of the door to enter their destination, *Forward Deck*. The *Forward Deck* is the hub of social activity on the station. It has several Bars, dance floors, live bands and restaurants.

As the Aero Lifts door opens they exit into the hustle and bustle of the social life of this station. Loud music is playing with the volume of the crowd's conversations nearly drowning out any way of hearing your conversation without raising your voice. A hostess, well endowed with long auburn hair greets Michael and Kathy, Michael: "Mr. Patel's suite please." At that the hostess calls an attendant over to escort Michael and Kathy through the crowd to a private, sound proof room with panoramic windows exposing both the forward lounge and behind the seating, space.

Upon entering the suite, smiles from ear to ear are on Michael and Pankaj.

Michael: "Pankaj! It's been too long, you look great!"

Pankaj grateful to see them, "You too my old friend, and Kathy, beautiful as usual. You keeping Mike out of trouble?"

Kathy smiled, "Far from it, it seems he enjoys trouble. I can't keep him out of it."

Pankaj laughs, "Indeed! Boy it's great to see you two. It's been way too long."

Michael more serious, "Twenty two years. How is Daksha and the girls?"

Pankaj, "Daksha is great. The girls are running up the school bills, both are in college and doing well. Thank you for asking. How about your kids?"

Michael grins, "They are here, Rebecca has grown up nicely and heads my security detail, still single, but we have hopes one day she will find someone. Russell too is well, our science officer he loves rocks and things, and Lizzy, too smart for her age. She tells me where to go and how to get there."

Pankaj laughing, "My kids in their own way tell me where to go and how to get there as well. Now what can I do for you two? What I have is yours you know that."

Michael, "You have always been a good friend since we were kids. I need your help when it comes to my current endeavor...."

Pankaj cuts him off "Xylon52?"

Michael with one eyebrow raised, "Not much of a secret I am afraid. The hopes for Earths technology may be contained on that planet. I am the only one with the technology to get there and retrieve the resources this planet needs if it is there at all. You are familiar with the Orion Syndicate?"

Pankaj, "Who isn't? He would love to have your warp drive schematics!"

Michael, "Exactly! As we speak his second in command is on this station and probably in this club waiting to talk to me, or worse."

Kathy gasps, "When were you going to tell me?"

Michael, "I just noticed him as we left the shuttle."

Pankaj, "I know Paul well. I wouldn't trust him as far as I could through him. He will offer you the moon and if you refuse, he will bury you in the moon. I heard Stan arrived, from what my sources tell me he will offer you the moon, and knowing you, you will deny that. Listen old friend, upon you leaving this station, he will collaborate with Rukkus and his security detail to intercept you before you can warp to your next destination."

Michael, "I realize that. I will meet with Stan and try to feel him out about their intercept plans. In the meantime I need your help to sabotage any advantage Rukkus' team may have in their launch."

Pankaj grins in a cheesy fashion, "Been awhile since we played outside. I think I can help you. Fortunately, Rukkus is hated and his team are a bunch of thugs. My connections within his organization will do as you need. Good luck! Best of journeys and a fruitful discovery on Xalon."

Michael, "Thank you! Say high to the family for me and your siblings."

Pankaj smiles, "I will. You know that with your escape here, Paul will hit the wall and put a bounty on your head that will span sector after sector."

Michael grins back "Yep, and may God help them when they meet the Phoenix."

With that, they stood up, with friendly hugs Michael and Kathy left Pankaj as he immediately got on the telecom to whoever he needed to talk to. From silence to the roar of a crowded night club, Michael and Kathy surveyed the crowd looking for Stan Whittaker, Kathy caught sight of him first sitting at the bar looking in their direction. Michael and Stan's eyes locked, Michael nods his head in one direction where they both make their way through the crowd to meet.

A quick handshake and Michael leads Stan to a secluded table, all the time Pankaj was observing the interaction through a closed circuit camera system on his desk. Busy on the telecom simultaneously, Pankaj observes the discussion knowing his old friend is in grave danger.

Stan, Kathy and Michael sit at a round table against a window into space, not as loud here but not quiet either.

Michael, "Fancy meeting you here."

Stan sarcasticly, "Thank you, I didn't think I was wearing fancy clothes."

Michael grins, "What is this all about?"

Stan, "You know why I am here. The warp drive schematics of course. Mr. Orion is willing to have you name your price no matter how high you may think it is."

Kathy stares coldly at Stan, Michaels mouth goes to one side then says "You guys don't quit do you? Stan, you and I have had this discussion over and over again. I want this technology to help mankind, your boss would simply extend his reach of illegal trade and rape more planets of their resources."

Stan shakes his head, "No! You have him wrong, he intends to help the Earth like you want to."

Michael interrupts him "For what price?"

Stan, "Expenses have to be offset like any good business."

Kathy sitting back still gazing at Stan knowing this was a line of BS. Orion's offset has cost the lives of millions all for the love of money.

Michael, "I see. What if I say no deal?"

Stan, "He will be very disappointed, so much so that he may do something to your ship and family I would regret."

Michael with a smirk, "You huh? I am sure he wouldn't regret it. What do you think honey?"

Kathy angrily, "Take your best shot you worthless piece of scum!"

Stan shaking his head, but not surprised at the outcome, "I am sorry, really I am. You give me no choice."

Kathy chastising him, "You have a choice, your just not man enough to make it!"

Michael holds Kathy's hand, "Let's go honey, we have to get ready for departure. Stan, I hope you can sleep with yourself at night. What is about to happen is partly on your head, blood will be on your hands, the future of mankind if we do not succeed will fall because of your bosses greed and your spineless observance of his orders. Let's go Kathy."

Chapter 4

Departure from Alpha One

Stan sits back in his chair as he sips from his cocktail as he contemplates what he must do next. “Rukkus? This is Stan Whittaker, initiate the Phoenix initiative.”

Rukkus, standing in his control room hangs up the comm. He types in the command for the initial assault on the Phoenix through a coded relay where four skilled military pilots are standing by. The four acknowledge the transmission and scurry to their fighters where they wait for the Phoenix to launch.

Back on the Phoenix the crew slowly returns with the goods and supplies needed for their mission.

Rebecca stands at the weapons array, Russell slips into his seat ready to relay any damage the ship may take. Lizzy plots their path through space to a safe jumping point. Zeeke is busy double checking all the instruments to make sure the Protonic containment system holds its own.

Michael: “We knew this was a possibility, and as you all are smart enough, you knew this will happen, not just this time but will probably happen again before our journey is through. Secure the hatch.”

Kathy presses a few buttons and the vacuum is heard through the walls of the ship.

Michael: "Release the docking clamps."

Kathy flips a switch while looking at her husband for reassurance. Michael gives her a half smile.

Michael with confidence in his voice, "Let's see what they got, leaving the hanger. Everyone keep a look out for our visitors."

The Phoenix slowly makes its way through the traffic of the hanger as Rukkus observes from the command deck of the station. Stan continues to sip on his cocktail waiting for the news that the ship has been disabled and captured. Pankaj, in his suite looking into space smiles with satisfaction over what he has planned.

As the Phoenix exits the hanger, Michael gives the command "Full impulse, shields up!"

As the ship clears the station the command to launch the fighters is given and they exit their launch tubes in lightning fast efficiency.

The leader of the squadron "Red One" gives his first order: "Side by side boys, arm your torpedo's and wait till your tracking system has a secure lock on the Phoenix." The ships lined up side by side in a tight formation, next we hear," Red two fire!", "Red four fire!" Two ships got a lock on the Phoenix well before the others, their torpedo's rushed from their underbelly and attained a lock on their target, but something is wrong, the ordinance is turning too sharply, they do an about face and start heading towards the ships that launched them.

Red One: "Evasive maneuvers!"

It was too late two ships were destroyed by their own torpedo and the concussion of the blast damaged Red Three.

Red Three "Captain, I have taken too much damage and can't launch."

Red One "Go back! I will finish this!"

Michael and his crew watched the entire drama unfold on the rear view screen, Michael with a smug smile "Thank you Pankaj, I owe you one."

Still there was one more bogie on his tail and boy is he mad.

Red One "Switching to manual targeting. O.K. Let's do this Old School." He pushes his yoke forward while pressing a button on the wheel causing his speed to accelerate and dive towards his target.

Michael "You see him Rebecca?"

Rebecca "Yes, I am tracking him now. He's pretty good."

Michael, "Hopefully not better than your old man." At that Michael pushed his controls down diving the ship while rotating it to come up in a half loop downward facing the opposite direction. The fighter was agile and was quick to compensate his flight path to match that of the Phoenix. Michael was moving the ship on all three axis to avoid the repeated shots from the fighter ionized canons. The yellow tracers whizzed by the ship with a few bouncing off its shields.

Rebecca, "Dad, shields are at ninety five percent. I almost have a lock."

Michael, "I am going to attempt the 'stop and go' procedure, hold on to your seats and stomachs!" At that he and Kathy pulled on two levers simultaneously to cause the ship to stand still in space, a hard brake. The fighter flew by them as they pushed those levers forward and the protonic engines screamed back into life and immediately started pursuit of the fighter.

Michael yells, "NOW BECCA!"

At that Becca locked on to the ship and released its death blow. The ship exploded in space and in its vacuum the fire was extinguished immediately.

Michael with relief, "Good job everyone! Now let's get the heck out of here before Rukkus sends back up."

Lizzy's hand furiously works on the control panel, "Dad, you have the coordinates for the first jump."

Kathy, "Got them!"

As the Phoenix rockets towards those coordinates the entire crew breathed a sigh of relief.

Michael, " Zeeke"

Zeeke, "Aye captain"

Michael, "Initiate the warp drive on my command."

Zeeke, “Aye, ready when you are captain.”

Michael, “Lizzy, ready?”

Lizzy, “Look on your screen.”

Michael, “Got them! Zeeke, initiate the warp drive!” With that command, the space around the Phoenix started to distort, pull and stretch in a surreal way until it simply collapsed around the ship and a whole new constellation was around them.

Lizzy, “Successful jump! We are now in the Capricornus constellation with Earths Twin star HIP102152 dead ahead.”

Two hundred and fifty light years in seconds, that is why Orion wants this technology. Space becomes a lot smaller in a twinkling of an eye. It never gets old, changing the sky like you would a shirt.

Chapter 5

Acatia

The crew is summoned to the strategy room where they all find their place at the table.

Lizzy, “I have plotted our path to *Sentient 521* as per your request Captain.”

Michael, “Thank you! The locals call this planet Acatia. I would like to prepare all of you not to be shocked as to what you will see here, varying degrees of humanoid and non-humanoid species.

“The planet as you will see is a red giant with crimson vegetation, cerulean hills, red fields and trees that shoot upwards of one hundred and fifty feet with a large teal foliage.”

Rebecca enthusiastically, ”Sounds incredible!”

Michael, “Yes, but in those trees lives the top of the food chain, a type of bird called the Agle. This creature is large about a ten foot wingspan with claws that exerts a thousand pounds per square inch and it is equipped with razor sharp teeth and armor like scales. Not something to be trifled with.”

Longbow, “I would be gobsmacked at the sight of that creature!”

Michael, “We will be arriving at the trade post, the hub of social activity and commerce. The building is circular, first five levels are for entertaining the traders, we will go to the sixth level where you will see rooms designed for specific trading of goods."

Russell curiously asking, "What will we be selling?"

Michael smiles, "I am glad you asked. The reason I attained thirty eight hundred liters of liquefied helium was to get enough currency to operate in this system. The currency used in outlying sectors is called the Grama. We will sell our precious cargo to the Acatians for fifty gramas per liter. This is a reasonable amount per liter but will give us plenty of money to operate in these sectors."

Rebecca, "By now, Paul Orion has put a bounty on our heads."

Michael, "That is something we expected, every bounty hunter in the galaxy should be getting word of the price put on our heads. We should expect some trouble at every turn."

Rebecca, "We will be ready."

Longbow, "Bunch of wankers!"

Russell, "I will get the Helium in a 'to go' box for you dad."

Michael with a small smile, "Thank you! Let's prepare for landing, Rebecca and Longbow, you will accompany me on the away mission just in case of any surprises." At that they all rose and went to their stations to prepare for a planetary landing.

Acatia is the fourth planet from their sun and has a gravity much like Earths, it is the size of Jupiter but as red as Mars. Michael strapping into the command chair gives the order to start the entry into Acatias atmosphere "Rotate forty degrees, elevate nose to thirty degrees, shields up, prepare for atmospheric burn."

At that command everyone was busy pushing buttons and pulling levers as the ship started its descent into Acatias stratosphere. The Phoenix was glowing red hot, flames encircled it as space and stars were replaced by a glowing red sunset, cumulous clouds glowing orange and the Phoenix bursting through them with thunder from its sonic boom.

Lizzy alertly, "I have patched landing coordinates to you dad, we have permission to dock on pad twenty, north east section of the hub."

Michael focused intently at the horizon and Kathy monitoring the gauges their hands grasping a quivering yoke to control the ship, Kathy flips a few switches and pulls on a lever to slow down their descent. Michael maneuvers the foot pedals to orientate the ship over the docking hub and fires the landing thrusters to ease the ship to her resting place. Dust and smoke bellow from beneath the Phoenix, all four hundred and fifty feet from stem to stern comes to a rest. Her wings jet upwards like a bird of prey, her belly shines like polished sterling silver, her wing tips sparkle like gems in a gold ring, a beautiful ship and worthy of her name and creator.

Kathy: "Down Captain and ready for departure."

Michael: "Excellent. I will try to get home before curfew."

Kathy: "You better! Last time we were here those Acatian bar maids wanted to experiment with interspecies breading."

Michael laughed, "They just don't measure up to you honey."

Kathy laughed, "That's an obvious they are only four and a half feet tall."

Michael grinned and at that, they rose from their seats where Michael met Rebecca and Longbow by the exit hatch. Michael "You ready?"

Rebecca: "I got my party favors and am ready to party."

Longbow: "You Americans are a strange bunch, Ready sir."

Michael: "Let's go make a deal. We will stand out since Zeeke, Kathy and I are the only Humans any of these creatures have ever seen. So no use in trying to hide just keep your cool, some of the patrons can seem rude or confrontational, but that's just the way they are."

Rebecca: "So, their Italian?"

Michael laughed, "Just pretend we are at a family reunion and your Uncle Nick is drunk."

"Good times!" Rebecca expressed sarcastically.

The three of them walked down long corridors that lead to a center circular hub with three other corridors branching from it leading to other landing pads, much like an airport on Earth. The hubs structure looks like a volcano with windows for each level as the three of them get closer the volume increases with each step, a strange music is playing and the unintelligible voices of the patrons increasing with every step till finally they enter the circular multi story room.

The commerce building and social hub has a center column that goes straight up to the sixth floor, around the column is Acatian's tending bar. Acatian's are short bi-pedal humanoids with blue hair, sunburnt red skin and large fore arms that would give Popeye a run for his money. Wearing brightly colored synthetic clothing despite their shortness they stand out in the bar. Along the perimeter tables encircle the center post and a dance floor between the tables and the bar with barmaids tending to the patrons.

Michael: "The Bar Boss is "Arbor" he has a Napoleon complex. We will talk to him to arrange an appointment for our trade."

Rebecca and Longbow's eyes grow big with the new sights and sounds that are around them. Trying to look cool and unaffected they walk behind their captain keeping their senses tuned into any possible trouble.

As they make their way up to the second level terrace, Michael finds a table for them to sit at, all the while every eye in the joint is fixated on them.

Longbow: "I do believe they are taking a piss at us."

Michael: "I don't think they are making fun of us but rather curious speculation."

Rebecca and Longbow have fire arms holstered to the sides and hidden knives and fighting instruments at the ready. They both have their right hands close to their sides just in case things go south quickly.

Michael: "At ease you two. I have been here before and as of now all looks normal."

Rebecca: "Strange definition of normal!"

A bar maid approaches the table, just over four feet tall, perfectly proportioned woman with red skin and blue hair she asks in her tongue for our order. Michael politely replies in her tongue something then all of a sudden she starts speaking English. "Thank you for the courtesy of turning on the translator." Michael politely said.

The bar maid, "For you honey, anything you want." She said with a smile.

Rebecca immediately shows her discomfort at the flirtatious munchkin.

Michael: "Mina, I would like to introduce you to my daughter Rebecca and her associate Longbow."

Mina: "It is a pleasure to meet you, been far too long since a human has graced us with their presence." As Mina surveys Longbow from head to two, "I didn't know humans came in a different color."

Longbow feeling her gaze undressing him simply returned her smile with a grin and said "several colors, I just happen to be the best color."

Mina smiles sheepishly "What can I get the three of you?"

Michael: "we will have a glass of Algarian Ale and please have Arbor come over and visit for a moment, I have a request."

Mina: "Lovely. Algor is at the bar and will relay your request." As she turns her gaze surveys Longbow one more time.

Michael with a grin "Looks like she likes you Longbow."

Longbow: "Your wife was right about these bar maids."

Through the crowd they can see Mina at the bar talking to another Acatian, he takes the tray of drinks from her and heads to the table to greet the three of them.

Arbor: "I thought I would bring you your drinks."

Michael: "It is good to see you again Arbor."

Arbor: “And I you kind sir. Mina said you wanted to see ma about a “request”?”

Michael: “Yes, I have something to trade and need to go to the commerce level to negotiate the trade.”

Arbor: “Human trading? I am curious. I can arrange a trade for a piece of the revenue.”

Michael knowing that Arbor is a business man and a greedy little guy sets up this small negotiation, “How big a piece?”

Arbor: “Ten Percent.”

Michael smiles staring into Arbors eyes, “Ten huh? I happen to know that your price for arranging trades is substantially lower than that. You must have a low opinion of humans or is it just me?”

Arbor grins, “No sir! Not at all, one must have a starting point to begin negotiations.”

Michael: “Start lower and we will see what we can come up with.”

Arbor grimaces not knowing that this human had knowledge of his normal price of two percent, “Five percent!”

Michael sits quietly, leans back in his chair and stares directly into Arbors eyes. Michael raises one eyebrow in silence. The men silently trade stares.

Arbor: “You are a stubborn human!” giving a growl he continues, “Two percent! That’s my final offer.”

Michael lowers his eyebrow and with a straight face, “Thank you for honoring my race with an equal and fair commission for our trade. What you didn’t realize is that this transaction is a large sum and you my friend will be paid handsomely for this arrangement.” Arbors grimace turns into a smile.

Arbor: “Drinks are on the house!”

At that small gesture Arbor heads toward the bar to attend to his usual affairs. Mina approaches a few minutes later, eyeing Longbow but addressing Michael, “Your meeting is scheduled in thirty of your earth minutes, is that satisfactory?”

Michael with a nod of approval, “Yes, thank you Mina.”

Mina with a light touch to Longbows forearm, “It is my pleasure and could be yours too.” Mina gives a wink to Longbow and walks as seductively as she could back through the crowd.

Meanwhile, while these arrangements were being made two Antorians entered the complex. Also bipedal humanoid, albino and hairless Antorians stand out too in a crowd standing on average about six foot six. These two wore leather attire with weapons strapped to their body like Rambo in a bad movie. One has blue eyes the other brown. They look so similar that the family resemblance was unmistakable. These two headed straight to the bar on the first level and had a seat. There they sat nursing a drink and talking to each other but saying little else to anyone around them.

Mina approached the table where Michael, Rebecca and Longbow sat, “You seem to be popular today.”

Michael: “What do you mean Mina?”

Mina: “There are two Antarians asking about you and your ship.”

Rebecca leans forward with an inquisitive look, “What can you tell us about the Antarians.”

Mina: “Well lovely, they are called the “Mad” brothers, one is called Gunner and the other Hunter. They are bounty hunters from Antaria and have connections through many sectors. Do you have a price on your heads?”

Michael leans forward with a grin, “Now Mina, who would want to pay for a human?”

Mina with a wide smile, looking at Longbow, ”I see one I would pay for.”

Michael: “Keep me apprised on what the Mad brothers are asking and any information you can give me about them will be handsomely compensated.”

Mina gazing at Longbow, “Handsomely? mmmm.” Longbow adjusting his collar feels like a piece of meat in a singles bar.

Longbow rolling his eyes, “Bloody Hell! That would be a dodgy night.”

Michael looks down at his watch and notices they should be making their way up to the sixth floor where the commerce area is. They sipped their last sip of their drinks and headed up the stairs trying not to catch undue attention so the Mad brothers wouldn't notice. Rebecca and Longbow kept one eye each on the albinos at the bar on the lower level.

Entering the commerce level, it is separated by offices of commerce, offices for Ore, Mineral, Gems, Commodities, Consumables and Helium. Helium in these parts is valued and fetches a good price. The three of them head over to the Helium office and enter.

The trading officer is an Acatian named Baron, standing up to welcome his guests, "Welcome humans! What can I do for you today?"

Michael: "We have cargo we would like to sell, thirty eight hundred liters of Liquefied Helium."

Baron with a poker face, "Helium is in good supply nowadays, I will give you thirty five gramas per liter."

Michael was familiar with the trading practices of the Acatians, saw this as a bold face lie, knowing that Helium is in short supply and is well worth much more than the fifty per liter he wanted for it. "I am sorry to waste your time, I will travel to Angoria and sell it to them." Angoria and Acatia are bitter rivals.

Baron with a perturbed look on his face, "Let's not be too hasty! I am sure we can come up with an agreeable price for your cargo."

Michael: "Yes, I am sure we could. Let's say sixty per liter."

Baron with a look of surprise and disgust, "Oh no! That is way too high for me, I am a simple business man and need to make a profit that can feed my family. I will go up to forty five per liter and that's my final price!"

Michael eyes the little man on the other side of the desk, stands up "good day then, I won't go below fifty per liter, and since that is your final price then I will go my way." He motions to Rebecca and Longbow to turn and upon turning he is stopped.

Baron stands up with his hands on the desk, "FIFTY! And that's my final offer!"

Michael turns around "Deal! I have it ready for pick up at my ship and two percent of this transaction goes to Arbor downstairs the rest you can deposit in my Bonthan bank account. It has been a pleasure doing business with you Baron."

Baron, knowing he just got out negotiated but still will is making a lot of gramas on this transaction returns the thank you to Michael with a grin. "You will see the gramas in your account as soon as we take receipt of the goods."

Michael: "Good day sir."

Michael, Rebecca and Longbow exit the office and make their way downstairs where they notice the Mad brothers are missing. Upon entering level two, Mina approaches them "The Antorians heard of your presence here and have made their way back to their ship, I am afraid they have something very unpleasant for you."

Michael: "Thank you Mina." Handing Mina ten gramas, she smiles and then pats Longbow on the backside before walking away. Longbow tried to pull away, then rolls his eyes with a grin.

Chapter 6

The Bounty Hunters

Michael with one eyebrow up looks at Rebecca, "Good news travels fast in space. Orion must have pushed this bounty through subspace channels with lightning fast efficiency. Let's get back to the Phoenix, but keep your senses sharp, we have quite a bit of open ground to cover from here to there. I am not sure what these Antorians have in mind but I am sure it is capture the ship and dispose of the crew."

Michael presses a button on his watch to open a com while walking back to the ship, "Kathy?"

Kathy: "Kathy here, did all go as planned?"

Michael: "Yes, um kinda. We should be expecting the Acatians to pick up the cargo within minutes and perhaps some unexpected visitors."

Kathy: "Unexpected?"

Michael: "Yes, two Antorian bounty hunters are here and on to us, secure the ship and organize the transfer of helium robotically. I want to make sure all are safe until we get back."

Kathy with a slight worry in her voice, "Will do. Be careful you three. Antorians are pretty brutal, they operate without a conscience. We will see you soon. Phoenix out!"

Rebecca and Longbow check their gear as Michael pats his holster; they were ready for this surprise but didn't expect it so soon.

Days on Acatia are long and the sun is still setting on the horizon, the sky burns in reds and orange while the trees reach for the heavens and become silhouettes against the sky. You can hear an Agle in the distance, a screaming sound, almost like a woman is being attacked. The sound created an eeriness to a beautiful backdrop. As they enter the open field they stay close to the side buildings just in case they need to take cover, the Phoenix is visible in the distance, looks like they may make it, suddenly a red tracer hits the ground just in front of them and explodes the vegetation leaving a gaping hole, the concussion is felt and nearly knocks the team over. Rebecca pulls Michael to cover behind the building.

They are about two hundred meters from the Phoenix, another red tracer just misses the building they are behind. All three pull their weapons having them at the ready. They try to calculate where the shots are coming from, another red tracer comes toward them and hits the side of the building with a loud bang as the building shutters. The shots originate too far for their hand held weapons to reach. Michael comes up with a plan, presses the comm button on his watch, "Kathy?"

Kathy: "What the heck is going on out there?"

Michael: "Surprise! We have that company we spoke of and they are out of range of our weapons." At that another tracer hits the ground at the corner of the building knocking up dust, Michael coughed, "Use the sensors to pin point the Antorians and send them a present from the Phoenix."

Kathy with urgency in her voice, "Will do, just don't get shot!"

Michael: "Really? O.K. I will take your advice this time."

Kathy hits the comm for Russell, "Russell! Get a pin point on the origination of the shots being fired and relay that to me at the helm."

Russell: "Working on it, almost got it........THERE! Sent to you."

Kathy see's the coordinates and works the targeting array to send a round of energy beams from their Gatling guns to the area. Yellow beams fly from the Phoenix toward the tall brush where the Antorians are nesting, the area lights up with fire as the spread of energy beams blanket the area.

The three of them watch as the Phoenix fires her shots and then wait to see if anymore fire comes from the brush towards them. Rebecca breaks the silence, "Looks like we at least have them pinned or they may have retreated, let's go quickly!"

Running from building to building no more shots were heading their way, they finally make a dash for the

Phoenix' gang way and enter the ship. Kathy was there to greet them, "I thought you need some fireworks for making the sale." She said with a grin.

Michael: "Thanks honey, did the cargo get delivered?"

Kathy: "Yes, transfer went well and the money is in our account."

Michael: "Awesome! Now everybody to their stations, it's time to leave this rock." He then gives the command to seal the hatches, fire thrusters as they took off for deep space.

Rebecca: "Well, they are a tough bunch."

Michael: "They?"

Rebecca: "Antorians."

Michael shook his head, "Where are they?"

Rebecca: "just leaving the planet, I think they didn't like our fireworks."

Michael: "They have no appreciation of a good light show. Full impulse and head toward the Antorian nebula."

Lizzy: "Antorian Nebula trajectory is laid in and on the helm!"

Michael focuses on the path he needs to follow and increases speed, "Time to play hide and seek. Russell! I need you to adjust our sensors to compensate as much of the Nebulas interference out as humanly possible."

Russell: "Aye Captain. I can give you what I can give you, the Nebula will make this difficult."

Michael: "Do your best. I need to see these two to hit them."

The Phoenix races toward the multi colored phenomena in space as the Antorian ship gives chase. The Antorian ships are semicircular with thrusters on the flat side and the helm dead center on the front curvature, their weapons fire from an array on the dome top and bottom. They are fast and agile.

Chapter 7

Hide and Seek

The Antorian Nebula is vast, twice the size of Acatia the planet they just left. The ultraviolet radiation ionizes the surrounding gas making it illuminate with a greenish color in space. Nebulas are seldom dense but in this case it is fog like and more importantly the radiation disrupts many propulsion designs and disrupts tracking systems. It is ironic that they are planning to defeat these bounty hunters in their own Nebula. This particular Nebula has an asteroid belt hiding within its fog thus making it more hazardous to enter. The Antorian Nebula is made up of Hydrogen and Helium gases, thus causing possible combustion if one does not engage properly in battle. The Phoenix is more than capable to navigate this phenomena with hopes that the Antorian ship will have problems making its way through.

Russell: "Captain, we are entering the Nebulas influence now."

Michael: "Zeeke copy?"

Zeeke: "Copy captain!"

Michael: "The protonic reactor may need some babysitting while we are in this nebula, the anti-protons simply don't react well to this radiation."

Zeeke: "Tell me something I don't know! I will sit on the baby captain, you can rely on that."

Rebecca: "Captain, I will ready the cold fusion torpedos to avoid Hydrogen detonation within the cloud."

Michael: "Smart move. Although I have another idea if we can get the cat to chase the mouse to its trap." As he says with a smug grin. Rebecca and the crew have an inquisitive look at that statement.

Rebecca: "The Antorians are entering the Nebula a thousand meters off our bow."

Michael: "Copy! Ready a spread of those torpedos in the rear tubes. Shields up!"

Rebecca: "Copy!" Seconds go by in silence as the whir of the engines are in the background, then suddenly BOOM! BOOM! The Antorians are sending what is the equivalent to depth charges hoping to get lucky. The explosions are close enough to shake the ship gently.

Michael sits in his seat with a silly grin, "adjust heading to eighty degrees starboard. Fire those torpedos!" The sound of the ordinance leaving the hull is a swoosh and seconds go by until a distant flash is seen on the radar and static field view screen. "That should get their attention!" Rebecca still has an inquisitive look not knowing what her father has planned. "Get us close to that large asteroid and make sure they follow."

Lizzy: "Aye, Aye Captain!"

As the Pheonix leads the Antorians through the Nebula, the Antorians continue to release more ordinance hoping to hit their prey. The Phoenix is jerked from time to time with near misses until they arrive to the asteroid. Michael leans forward grabbing the controls, "Charge up Impulse beam canons!"

Rebecca: "Are you sure? They may set off the hydrogen!"

Michael with a grin and full focus on the static filled screen, "I realize that, charge them up!" The Phoenix navigates to the far side of the asteroid away from the Antorians, "forty five degrees port, full impulse!" The ship turns sharply and accelerates away from the asteroid, at that the Antorian ship hugging the asteroid makes its way in view, "Target the asteroid! FIRE IMPULSE RAY!" At that command Rebecca presses a button and the yellow beam heads toward the large asteroid hitting it squarely behind the pursuer's ship, the asteroid detonates like a large nuclear bomb and destroys the Antorian ship with a concussion wave felt on the Phoenix.

Rebecca: “What happened?”

Michael: “That asteroid had a small oxygen environment and when we ignited it with our impulse beam it ignited the hydrogen around it, what you saw was essentially a hydrogen bomb cooked up in the last minute.” He leans back in his chair and smiles, “Not too shabby of a science experiment.”

Smiles of satisfaction come across the crews faces. Michael gives the command, “Let’s get out of this cloud and fly to our next jump point.

Lizzy: “Aye Aye Captain!”

Chapter 8

The *Phoenix*

The Phoenix initiated the warp drive, space stretched, bends and then collapses around the ship propelling it to the next set of stars in the sky, the *Keplar* system; six hundred light years from Earth.

Michael leans back and hits the comm button, “We have a few days travel in this sector before we rendezvous with an ally ship the *Eaglefire*. I would take this time to regenerate ourselves before any more action happens.”

Michael sets the autopilot on the helm to arrive at a set of coordinates he has arranged with the *Eaglefire,* a large combat carrier and flagship of the Yag Alliance. The Yag Alliance is the largest and most influential in this and neighboring sectors. It is made up of over one hundred planets. The Phoenix and her crew will meet with Primus the leader of the Yag and negotiate entry into their alliance. This will protect the Phoenix from Orion and his minions.

The Phoenix is a medium size ship in space of only three hundred and fifty meters in length. Her fuselage is suspended above her outstretched wings at the tip of the glow with the fire of her protonic propulsion.

The main body of the Phoenix has five levels, the first level is engineering, second is crew quarters, third is science, sickbay and recreational areas, the fourth is the galley, strategy room and astrophysics then finally the fifth level is the helm and bridge. Each level is accessible via stairs or Aero Lifts located fore and aft of the ship.

Lizzy of course thinks the Astrophysics lab is the recreational room. She could be found there studying the holographic maps of the solar systems and sectors. To her it is a game to try and name all parts of each map.

Rebecca and Longbow use the recreational room more than most although not the way most would, they will be found in the firing range where holographic targets are projected and they have to shoot them.

Zeeke, plays in the engine room, to him the Protonic Reactor and the Warp Drive are amusing through the detail and science of both. In the engine room which spans ninety meters long, fifteen meters wide and ten meters high, it is the largest cubic area room in the ship. The Protonic drive is an hour glass shaped housing some eight meters tall and seven meters wide. The engine uses Protons and Anti-Protons to create the necessary energy to not only propel the ship but also to generate enough power for the Warp Drive. Anti-Protons are gathered by shooting a high intensity proton beam at the Iridium thus creating the fuel we need to operate. Iridium is a very rare earth element and very expensive.

The warp drive is located fifty meters aft of the Protonic Reactor, it is seven by seven meters in size with cables from the top of the cylindrical device down to the large square base. The Warp Drive is connected to forward and rear arrays on the ships outer hull, when they are initiated the warping of space is initiated.

Russell, most of level three is his toy, loves science and is our doctor when need be. The science lab is chock full of goodies for him, from geological samples to organic ones, fun! Fun! Fun!

Michael and Kathy are a little simpler in their recreation, a game of pool or sipping a drink or reading a book in from of a window as they watch the stars go by.

The ten crew quarters are comfortable but not luxuriant; each quarter is equipped with a work station, off suite bathroom, bed and discussion area with chairs and a couch. The Captains Quarters is larger of course, a four room living space, bathroom, bedroom, kitchen and living room.

Since Michael and Kathy are from an older generation than the youthful crew they have, food is prepared by hand instead of synthesized in a machine. Each crewman takes turns preparing meals for the team. Some day's it is even edible.

After all the excitement of this past week, the crew is enjoying some down time. Each day at ten hundred hours the crew gets together in the strategy room for updates and discussion about the future happenings of this mission.

The upcoming rendezvous with the *Eaglefire* is a primary topic. Primus is from the planet Elgar, the *Elgarians* are very similar to humans in appearance. Typically very muscular also experts in hand to hand combat due to their innate ability to read the minds of others. They literally know what punch you will through next. Their mind reading ability happens within a three meter area, thus useless in space combat.

Days in space have passed way too quickly; the rendezvous with the *Eaglefire* is this afternoon.

Chapter 9

The Eaglefire

The *Eaglefire* is a large carrier. Shaped like a plus sign, one thousand meters tall and twelve hundred meters wide. This ship holds thirty two fighters within its launch bays, each fighter wing is made up of eight fighters. The fighters are pattern in design like the carrier, seven by seven meters each. These are equipped with multiphasic weapons to punch through shields. The carrier itself has at the ends of each arm an array that will fire energy weapons in rapid succession. The bridge is located at the top of the center arm. The *Eaglefire* can travel at light speed. It is agile for a ship its size and has layered armor to protect against all kinds of ordinances. It is a BEAST!

It is ten hundred the morning of the meet, all are gathered in the strategy room as per custom.

Michael: “Today in approximately four hours will rendezvous with the *Eaglefire*. This is the flagship for the Yag coalition. I will meet with Primus, the leader of the coalition. Primus and I have had some dealings in the past and have collaborated on a few joint ventures.”

Rebecca: “What ventures?”

Michael: "That's not important now except to say we have gotten to respect each other's viewpoint on matters. We need the Yag Coalition to back us up and embrace the Phoenix and its crew to protect us against any that dare to reap the bounty on our heads. Nobody! Dares to take on the Yag. I have secured enough money and or Iridium to help us in negotiations."

Rebecca: "After this is negotiated, will we be heading to Xalon52?"

Michael: "Yes. Now if there are no questions let's get ready to meet our future alliance."

The Eaglefire loomed before the Phoenix like a tidal wave in front of a fishing boat. Fighter wings are flying in formation to the left and right of the beast.

Michael: "Eaglefire, copy?"

Eaglefire: "Copy."

Michael: "The Phoenix request permission to enter the hanger bay."

Eaglefire: "Permission granted, hanger bay two left side."

Michael: "Copy, two left side, out."

The Phoenix approaches the behemoth and enters the left side of docking bay two. It looked like a giant star fish was gobbling up the small craft. Upon entering the bay the ship came to rest on support pylons a gangway tube was extended to the exit hatch where clamps secured it in place, air tight.

Michael: “Secured! Gangway pressurized. Well, let’s go visit an old comrade.” Looking at Kathy.

Kathy: “I hope he remembers you saved his life.”

Michael grins, “Tough to forget, but the Elgarians are not the generous type. Negotiations and deals must be made to get what we need from him. Rebecca, you are in charge of the bridge till we return”

Rebecca heading to the helm, “Aye, Aye Captain.”

At that the two of them headed to the exit and down the gangway to an open area where two Elgerian soldiers waited to greet them.

Soldier: “This way, Primus is waiting.”

Kathy and Michael followed the one soldier while the other followed close behind. The walk led them through the windows of the hanger bay where dozens of ships were docked, turning left they entered a larger corridor lined with lights and display screens with doors every three meters or so. Elgerians were seen going to and fro tending to the duties they were assigned. At the end of the corridor we entered an elevator, room enough for twenty or so people. The leading soldier pressed a button and we started to ascend up and up. The display screen on the wall was displaying the Elgerian language which looks like a bunch of wavy lines and periods.

The lifts doors opened to the command bridge where a looming figure was commanding orders from an elevated seat, Primus. Primus stands about six foot three, at two hundred and thirty pounds his muscular arms and wide shoulders should he had very little body fat on him. His hair is as black as space with ruby red eyes and his skin was tanned like he had just come from a coastal vacation. He turned around after his last order was given. "Mike! Kathy! It is good to see you!"

Michael with a welcoming smile, "It is good to see you too, been awhile."

Primus: "Come! Let's go to my ready room and we can talk of some of our adventures. Maul! You have the con!" At this, Primus leads them to a room off to the left of the bridge, doors slide open and they enter a beautiful room with a panorama window into space and chairs seated around a large oval table. "Please have a seat."

Michael: "Thank you. You are probably wondering why I have asked to see you."

Primus laughs, "No my old friend I am not. The bounty on your head is high, one million gramas. That would make anyone nervous and cause them to seek some shelter."

Michael: "Indeed! We have already had a couple run ins, and are hoping we could negotiate entry into the Yag Alliance."

Primus leans forward with a serious look, "Well, we have been busy in this sector. We have just finished warring with the Zurrians and came out with many losses. Fortunately, they too had many losses. We have negotiated a cease fire for the moment and it is tenuous at best."

Kathy: "Sounds like war is still looming."

Primus: "Perhaps, we will both lick our wounds to see what happens next."

Michael: "Does you telling us this story have a purpose?"

Primus: "Indeed it does. You and your crew are needed to rescue my officer from Zurria. They are asking for Iridium as a trade for his release."

Michael: "I see. I have iridium and by using us you keep your hands clean."

Primus: "Yes. Elgarians don't like leaving one of theirs behind and when you contacted me it was like fate."

Michael: "What do they need iridium for?"

Primus: "Not sure exactly, but our intel says they want to build a Gamma Ray device for battle. They have several planets they are disputing rights with and I am sure they are up to no good."

Michael: "Far be it for me to hand over the fuel for a weapon that destroys organic matter at the cellular level. We will have to get him out some other way."

Primus with a grin: "I knew you would see it my way. My intel is fairly good on where they are keeping "J". A planet with ninety percent of the surface covered in water, leaves very little left for us to guess about. I will see to it that you get all the information we have on Zurria and after you retrieve my officer, the alliance will defend any and all who dare to attack you."

Michael: "I would appreciate it if you can keep them off our backs while we rescue "J"."

Primus: "Indeed. Consider it done."

Primus hits a comm button and orders the head of security into the room where he will take point in downloading Zurrian files to Michael and Kathy.

Chapter 10

Rescue Plans

The Phoenix travels at light speed toward their destination the crew is meeting in the strategy room to discuss what is known about the Zurrians.

Michael: "First of all, the Zurrians are a crustaceous civilization, although they can walk upright they prefer to walk on six legs. They are a warrior race on a planet that is ninety percent water. The Zurrians live in cities under the oceans but they have a stockade on an island near their citadel. Each Zurrian when standing upright is about eight feet tall, their pincher arms extend far beyond their legs and are dangerously powerful. They have adapted laser weapons to their physique and are very adept at fighting in close quarters and from afar."

Rebecca: "Do we have intel on the stockade and the island?"

Michael: "Yes. The island is fairly small about ten square miles. It has a flat top with a dense forest hiding some surprises for us."

Longbow: "Bloody hell, what does the island have in store for us?"

Michael: "Several indigenous creatures we need to prepare to take on since we will be landing on the far side of the island. They too are crustaceous in nature, large one is the vampire and the other the spider crab. These two are deadly and the spider crab lives up to its name, it weaves steal like webs, when caught in it you are as good as dinner."

Russell: "I can make hand devices to cut your way through them."

Rebecca: "Excellent! We will need them. How far to the stockade from our drop off point?"

Michael: "Two miles. There will be barracks on the ledge above the stockade, we will have to either sneak by them or take them out."

Longbow: "I prefer to take them out. I am more a lobster man than a crab man."

Michael: "That will be a last resort. The stockade is below the cliff on another ledge, we will zip line down to the roof. The jail cells are on the top floor so once there we will blow a hole in the roof, drop down and extricate the prisoner."

Rebecca: "What is the exit strategy, we surely will be noticed by then?"

Kathy: "You are correct. I will swing the Phoenix around the island while providing cover and pick you up on the ledge where the stockade is. There will be enough room to land, you will zip line down to the ledge to where the Phoenix will be."

Michael: "While the Phoenix provides cover we will enter her belly and get the heck out of there."

Lizzy: "I am sure they won't let us go so easily."

Michael: "I agree. The Zurrians will launch a counter squadron to intercept us, we need to be at red alert and all weapons armed for a full defensive. So once aboard the Phoenix, all hands to their stations! Skirpach, their leader is a tenacious crustacean, he will give pursuit with a vengeance. "

Rebecca: "What do we know about the ship designs?"

Kathy: "Plenty! The Yag Coalition has just completed a war against them and their ships are formidable. The ship is in an "X" wing design with four rapid firing energy canons. They are swift and quick. They have shields designed for energy weapon defense."

Rebecca: "So a type of explosive or projectile weapon would be preferred in battle."

Michael: "Yes. This will not be easy as you can all see. We are more than capable of pulling this off. When we do we will meet back with the Eaglefire and deliver his officer."

Rebecca: "I will get the gear ready."

Michael: "Great! You, Longbow and I will be the rescue team on the ground and the rest here in the Phoenix. Any questions?" Concerned looks on everyone's face but all were silent. "Great let's get to preparation's, we arrive at Zurria tomorrow at twenty two hundred, get plenty of rest, we are going in at night."

Chapter 11

This Planet has Crabs!

Stars past by the Phoenix in streaks as she makes her way to Zurria where the team assembles the gear for the mission. Michael leaves the helm to Kathy and heads down to the armory where Rebecca and Longbow are.

Michael: "How are we coming along?"

Rebecca and Longbow are checking gear and assembling the belts and the backpacks need for the three of them.

Rebecca: "Almost ready. What do we know about the Zurrians exoskeleton and its weak areas?"

Michael: "Like most crustaceans we need to aim for the joints where there is soft tissue. Our aim and must be precise. Since we are going in under the cover of night, we will rely on our scanners to detect activity and guide us to our destination. Night vision won't help us much since crabs don't put off a heat signature, eyes, ears and our scanners are the only way we will be able to detect them."

Longbow: "We have to be a nutter to do this at night."

Michael: "I realize the risk, but the Phoenix needs the cover of darkness to drop us off and pick us up. She can avoid radar but not visual."

Longbow: “Bloody hell! I think we have everything except the loo.”

Michael chuckles, “You better go before the mission then.”

Longbow: “Damn straight!”

Michael: “We are almost there, I will meet you two at the hatch as soon as we land.”

Michael makes his way up to the bridge where Kathy, Russell and Lizzy are at their posts. Michael makes his way next to Kathy at the helm. “I can see that our stealth running is activated.”

Kathy: “Roger! Better safe than sorry. I wasn’t sure how far out they could detect us. I have been flying behind moons and planets to avoid visuals from their patrols.”

Michael: “Awesome! A little hide and seek huh?”

Kathy: “Not as much fun as that but it is effective.”

Kathy: “Lizzy?”

Lizzy: “Copy Captain. Landing coordinates are on your nav screen.”

Kathy: “The team ready?”

Michael: “Yes,”

Kathy: “Nervous?”

Michael: “What’s there to be nervous about? Landing on a strange planet in the dark with crablike monsters we can't see until they are on top of us, piece of cake!"

Kathy: "At least the moons are full, they should give you some light."

Michael: "Some anyways."

Kathy: "We are entering the stratosphere; you better get down there with the team. Take care and come back to me in one piece."

Michael: "How do you like your crab cooked?"

Kathy: "Ha! Ha! Now go and be a hero."

Michael gets up from his chair leans over and kisses Kathy on the cheek. "Don't forget to pick me up."

Kathy smiles, "Only if you succeed."

Michael: "Ha, Ha! See you soon."

At that Michael makes his way down to the exit hatch where Rebecca and Longbow are waiting. Each with gear strapped to their sides and light backpacks. Knives, guns, grappling hooks and zip line equipment along with their scanners and communication gear. Each is wearing headgear that displays topography in front of them and imbedded in the gear are two way communicators. Although they won't be able to see heat signatures of the enemy they can still navigate the terrain. They hope to see disruptions in the imaging to capture the outlines of any ingenious life forms they may encounter.

Kathy enters Zurria's atmosphere some two hundred miles from the landing point, flying low over the water at a snail's crawl for this ship, two hundred fifty miles per hour. The Phoenix is skimming over the tops of the waves, the water is black from night with reflections of the three moons flying high overhead.

Lizzy: "Target dead ahead, fourteen miles at twenty degrees starboard."

Kathy: "Copy that." Her attention focused squarely on the telemetry screen. The ship has a heads up display for flying blind; she zeroes in on the target and eases the Phoenix to it. She fires the landing thrusters on a clearing just outside the dense forest. The Phoenix comes to a safe and gentle landing. "All clear, seems step one is completed. Opening the hatch! Good luck and come home safe!"

Michael: "Have the hot water boiling, we will bring home the crabs." After that sarcastic statement, the three of them exit the ship to see the hatch close immediately behind them. The ship will stay there until they signal for extraction.

As they step onto the rock soil of Zurria, the light of the moons illuminate the tops of the trees as the bases of which plunge into darkness. The sound of the Phoenix' engines cooling off lowers to a quiet hush. Clicks and squeals emanate from the forest ahead of them. Seeing a path thirty degrees to their right through their heads up display they make their way to it and enter the darkness of a dense forest.

The trees are huge, like sequoias back on planet earth. The tops though spread out and create a canopy, so dense it nearly blocks out all the moon beams. Small beams of the light of the moon are shooting through to the ground from what little openings there are in the canopy. The ground is thick with leaves and brush, the vegetation on the ground is unforgiving. Longbow leads the way with a machete hacking at the outgrowth making a path for the three of them. His arms swing tirelessly as the other two keep an eye out for any disruptions in the displays.

Clicks grow louder, longbow stops swinging the machete and stands still. “I saw something.” He mutters.

Rebecca: “Details?”

Longbow: “Yellow illumination twenty degrees left one hundred feet ahead.

All three stare into the forest at those coordinates, then, two yellow eyes become visible.

Michael: “Vampire crabs!” Remember soft tissue. “Where there’s one there are dozens.” Adrenalin starts to flow more rapidly through their bodies as they go right hoping to avoid the creatures.

Longbow leads the way with phaser pistols drawn, Rebecca aiming left of Longbow and Michael aiming right of him. Soon eyes started to appear in a large number to their left, still as if they were watching us yet not engaging. Longbow continues to hack faster and harder as both pistols are centering their sights between the eyes of any target they could.

Suddenly the yellow glow of their eyes start to spread out, some going up the trees and the others encircling the three of them. Longbow stops dead in his tracks and draws a grenade from his belt.

Michael in a steady purposeful tone, “Wait for them.” Seconds ticked by like minutes, minutes like hours, the three of them have their backs to each other all facing a different direction, then, the crabs started to approach in a hurry. “NOW!”

Michael and Rebecca fire into the night, fire erupts from the foliage, Longbow released one hand grenade and then another, the ground explodes. The yellow eyes start to extinguish one after another, above them more in the tree tops start their assault. Longbow grabs his rifle and fires what can be described as a shotgun blast into the air with blue energy tracers.

One crab from above falls at their feet; the creature is six feet across with a crimson red shell and those yellow eyes dark. Others start falling form the trees as the wide spread of the gun hits one after another.

Rebecca continues to target with incredible accuracy the advancing line of crabs. Michael reaches into his belt and grabs a round ball, he hits a button and blades protrude from it. He releases the device by throwing it in the direction of the crabs, looking down at his watch he controls the drone towards the army of crabs. The drone is equipped with razor sharp spinning blades enhanced by extreme heat the blades cut through organic material with ease. The drone starts left and then goes right as it severs the legs of each and every crab until the remaining retreat.

Michael: “Crab legs anybody?”

Rebecca shaking her head at the bad joke, “Daaad!”

Longbow: “Bloody hell! Couldn’t you have done that earlier?”

Michael with a grin, “Now what’s the fun in that? Too bad we don’t have a doggy bag.”

Rebecca rolls her eyes at her father’s puns.

Chapter 12

The Rescue

The three push through the forest, the moons move slowly through the night sky. Days on Zurria are about thirty six hours long. The night envelopes them as the moon beams shoot through the tree tops, Longbow continues without let up, leading the way and clearing the vegetation. Short shrills are heard along with a cricket like background. Rustling in the trees overhead make the three of them look sharply. With adrenalin still pumping through their veins from the vampire crab battle, they push through until they come to a small clearing. Longbow holds up his open palm as to signal halt.

Michael whispers, “What is it?”

Long bow: “I saw something disrupt my display. Wait.” A few seconds go by, “There it is again! Do you see it, dead ahead in the clearing.”

Both Michael and Rebecca gaze forward and see something disrupting the topography and moving slowly.

Michael in a low tone, “Copy that. Spider crabs?”

Rebecca: “They are big enough.”

Longbow shows frustration on his face, “How in the bloody hell are we to travers this without tackling those monsters?”

Michael: “We are getting too close to the barracks to use energy weapons without causing an alarm of some type. We stay in a tight triangle and work our way along the perimeter trying to stay concealed in the vegetation, watch out for what may look like static on your displays.”

Rebecca: “Why? What will that mean?”

Michael: “Spider webs! Although we can cut our way out, we may not have enough time to do it. Those things have a stride of fifteen feet and would be on us too quickly. The plasma torches Russell made for us may give us a short cut through the webbing slowing down the pursuers. The webbing may act as a type of wall giving us time to escape.”

Longbow: “Why don’t you use that food processor drone?”

Michael: “I will, not to worry. It seems if we do engage them the drone will be a silent way to dispose of them, remember no explosions.” Rebecca seems disappointed at that last statement.

The glade was about fifty meters in diameter as the three of them slowly made their way around the perimeter staying low with Michael at point. Rebecca whispers ahead, “webbing at two o clock.”

Michael: “Copy. Status of our friends?”

Longbow: “Chatting among themselves from what I can gather.”

Michael continues to guide them through the tall grass, Rebecca breaks the silence, “Dad! One is making it’s way toward us, must have heard our footsteps.”

Michael holds his palm up motioning them to halt. All eyes were fixed on the dim image of a large spider crab illuminated by the moons beams. The predator was heading to their right where they had just been. The crab makes a series of clicks and two more come to its location. Michael motions with his hands to follow him into the jungle, they do as they are commanded while keeping an eye on the three crabs. A twig snaps under the weight of Longbows boot, the crabs stand still with a sudden jerk of what you can call their head they peer into the jungle directly at the three of them.

Michael stands up “HURRY! This way!” Immediately they start running following the captain closely, Michael reaches into his backpacks side pocket and pulls out the plasma torch, Rebecca and Longbow follow suit.

The crabs start their pursuit traversing grown faster than one could imagine. The three of them reach the webbing and start to cut it individually to make one single hole, they rushed through it, still running as fast as they can through the jungle.

The crabs reach the webbing and take the long rout of scaling it and coming up the backside to continue their pursuit.

Longbow was bringing up the rear, "Looks like we only have the three chasing us!"

Rebecca in full stride, "Dad, the drone!"

Michael reaches into his bag of tricks, presses the button on the drone and throws it over his left shoulder while running; he stopped to operate the controls. The drone starts to spin its deadly blades as Michael controls it to slice off the legs of the front pursuer, as that crab squeals in pain the other two stop to inspect the casualty. They restart their pursuit while the drone is commanded to take out the hind legs of the rear crab. Michael nervously states, "One more!"

Rebecca: "I would, um, hurry if I were you."

Michael: "Don't rush me good crab takes time to prepare." At that the drone hits the last crab, cutting its legs out from under it. The drone silently returns back to its owner.

Longbow with a sigh of relief, "You have some bollocks captain!"

Michael with a grin, "Let's go we are almost to the cliff. The barracks are about twenty meters left of our current position. Hopefully the crabs are tucked into their shells for the night."

Upon arriving at the edge of the cliff, they are overlooking the stockade building, octagonal about seven stories tall. Made of honed out stone, the facility will be difficult to access.

Rebecca reaches into her backpack and pulls out the grappling hook and loads it into the gun, she takes a steady aim at the wall just above the last level that probably houses the roof access stairway. She squeezed on the trigger without breaching and the hook launches making its way into the wall securing itself completely. She immediately ties her end to a tree for the three of them to descend upon the roof.

Michael then Longbow and finally Rebecca descend the zip line landing softly on the roof of the facility. Michael breaks out a scanner, as he walks on the roof, the scanner is looking for heat signatures through the rock. The scanners green indicator light illuminates, "Here!"

Rebecca makes her way over, "How thick is the stone dad?"

Michael: "eighteen inches give or take."

Rebecca calculates the right amount of power to the blue laser cutter. "Dad, how many are below us?"

Michael begins to do a wider scan, "Hmmm."

Longbow: "What is the hm about?"

Michael: "I see three prisoners and no gaurds."

Longbow: "Humph!"

Rebecca: "Looks like we might have a couple more guests."

Michael: "Indeed."

Rebecca starts the cutting of the roof as quiet as she could, the high intensity blue laser is cutting the roof like scissors to a piece of paper.

In the Jail, J is sensing a presence. It is above him. The ruggedly handsome Elgarian with his red eyes and brown hair is able to sense the rescue that is undergoing. He looks over to the two other prisoners, both female from the planet Shaya. “Wake up! Wake Up! Juliette, Kaira get up!”

The two slowly open their eyes and see a small blue laser cutting a hole in the roof.

Shayan’s are beautiful women scantily clad standing about six foot two in stature. Well-endowed with long legs these two brunettes would turn the head of any man on earth. Juliette is first to her feet, “What’s going on?”

J: “There are three humans above us, they are cutting a hole to aid us in an escape.”

Kaira: “Humans? What’s a human?”

Juliette: “Oh! Never mind her! I don’t care what they are as long as we get out of here.”

Rebecca continues the cut until it comes full circle, the large stone fragment drops with a loud thud. “That should have woke a few up, boy will they be crabby!”

Michael pressed a button on his comm to signal the Phoenix to hurry to the extraction point.

Michael grins at her pun, and drops a line. Longbow drops into the parallelogram shaped room and cuts the locks off of J's door. J urgently pleads, "I know you came here just for me but these two deserve to be rescued as well." Longbow seeing the concern in J's face he immediately cuts the locks off of the other two doors.

Longbow in haste says, "Hurry they will get here soon! Up the rope, NOW!" Longbow was the last to make it up to the roof at that moment the shrill of an alarm sounded.

Michael was there to help the prisoners up to the roof, lending a hand and pulling them up. "Hello ladies! We will save formal introductions till later, right now we need to go!"

Rebecca hurried over to the far side of the roof where she launched another grappling hook from the gun it landed on a tree securing their line on a pipe protruding from the roof they all strapped on their harnesses. The Shayan's had to hold tight to Michael and Longbow as they made their descent to the beach.

Energy beams were emanating from the cliff top where the barracks were and hitting the ground around them. The roof top started to join the party and shoot in wide bursts to the beach head, at that moment the Phoenix arrived and put its hull between the shooters and the rescue team. The Phoenix landed on the beach engaging her guns toward the shooters, a blistering pace of rapid fire shut down the Zurrian's quickly. The team made their way up the gangplank and into the safety of the ship. Quickly the hatch closed behind them, then Kathy raised the Phoenix over the stockade and blasted it with proton torpedos.

Michael hurried up to the bridge while Longbow tended to the guests, Rebecca hurried to her station the fight was just getting started.

Chapter 13

The Escape

In the Zurrian Citadel Skirpach hears of the prison break, raising his claws and screaming his order, "LAUNCH RED AND BLUE SQUADRONS, KILL THEM!" At that command the launch bays under the dark oceans tide launched two sets of eight ships. They rushed towards the surface and pushed through the waves like missiles being launched from a submarine. These two squadrons pulled into a tight triangle formation soon after hitting the air.

Michael making his way back to his seat next to Kathy, "I would have brought you some crab legs but Becca forgot to pack doggy bags."

Kathy smiled at his gesture, "Right now we have sixteen bogies inbound toward us."

Michael: "I see you thought ahead, red alert and shields, how nice." A smirk left her face. "Full impulse! I remember from the briefing there was a small continent not far from here, just chock full of canyons and waterfalls, feel like a romantic trip to a state park honey?" Again, Kathy gives him a smirk.

The Phoenix leads the way to the land mass with the fighters about two thousand meters behind still in their tight formation. Lizzy hails the captain, "Captain, land ahead!"

Michael smiles at Kathy, "Ready for a roller coaster ride?" He grabbed the controls while transferring the heads up display showing the topography on the view screen. "Look honey, a video game." He laughed. Slowing the Phoenix down enough for the fighters to close the gap; "Divert extra power to the rear shields!"

Rebecca: ""Aye! Aye! Captain."

Now comes the fun part Michael was thinking, passing over the land to a hostile topography, in the dark of night the heads up display was all he had to go by, mountains were outlined in green with elevation markers, they passed by the display too fast for an ordinary pilot to navigate. Michael though was enjoying this way too much.

Rebecca: "Incoming fire!"

Then suddenly, energy beams shot left and right of the Phoenix, some hitting her rear side. Michael slowed the Pheonix even more letting the pursuers gain more ground and have their weapons hit the ship with more frequency. Rebecca calls out, "Shields are at eighty percent!"

Michael: "Plenty of time!" As he rears the ship closer and closer to the pursuers, he suddenly turns the ship ninety degrees causing her to immediately fly sideways, he narrowly makes it through a rock mass archway where three of the pursuers exploded in a hail of fire and debris.

Rebecca: “Nice move dad! Thirteen to go.”

Michael smiles with wide eyes focused intently on the display, green lines pass quickly, elevation lines go up and down, the firm grip he has on the wheel along with Kathy adjusting the elevation of the ship shows how these two have such a happy marriage, they are in sync in what they do. The two act as one as they pilot the Phoenix through one hazard to another dropping one fighter then another fighter through the canyons of this alien landscape. Michael calmly gives out his next move, “We are about to hit open water, ready to become a submarine?” Michael and Kathy upon exiting the canyon to the beach dives the Phoenix toward the water and with a great splash and sudden jerk the ship dives to the depths of this ocean. The seven remaining fighters join them in the depths.

Michael: “I hope you all can swim. Prepare to release the mines and set the timer to manually detonate, Rebecca, when you see them fly over them honey...”

Rebecca: “I know, I get to blow something up.” As she said with a smile.

Michael: “On my mark.” “Now!”, “Now!”, “Now!”, “Now!” the mines dropped the under belly doors to float and rest on the oceans floor.

Rebecca eyed the radar and then, BOOM! BOOM! BOOM! BOOM! BOOM! BOOM! Smiling she exclaimed “Bogies are gone captain, we are free and clear.”

Michael: “Let’s see what space has to offer, stealth mode activated. Let’s get out of here.” The Phoenix rose from the ocean invisible to the Zurrian radar system, for all they could tell is that all ships, friend and foe were lost at sea.

Upon entering outer space Michael got up from his chair to greet his new guests. Rebecca, come with me please. They walked down to the lower level to sickbay where Russell was examining the rescued prisoners. "I hope you all are in good shape."

J: "We are captain, the Shayans and I were fairly well treated by the Zurrians."

Michael: "J, I expected to see you, but you two, well you are a surprise. Shayan huh! Where is your planet located?"

Juliette spoke first, "First of all we would like to thank you and your crew for our rescue, we will not forget such heroism. My name is Juliette and this is Kaira. Our planet is the fifth from this sun."

Michael: "Nice to meet you. My name is Michael, you have spent a little time with Longbow and this is my daughter Rebecca. Russell has been tending to your injuries if you had any. My wife Kathy is flying the ship right now and Lizzy is at the navigation station. Our engineer is Zeeke, he rarely comes up from out of his hole."

Kaira: "Captain, would you mind dropping us off on our planet?"

Michael: "I would be delighted to. I have never visited your planet. What would you like to tell me about it?"

Juliette: "We are a civilization of nothing but women with one exception, the Architect."

Longbow: "The Architect?"

J is sitting in his seat looking at Rebecca with a smirk, knowing the story already.

Juliette: "The Architect is the sole man, his purpose is to donate the necessary semen for us to genetically reproduce."

Longbow: "Bloody lucky chap!"

Michael with a grin, "Poor guy must be exhausted."

Juliette: "Although we have a queen, Omari, that rules Shaya, the Architect is treated like a King but has no authority."

Longbow: "Bloody lucky chap!"

Russell: "Are you saying he has sex with all of you?"

Kaira: "Sex?"

Russell: "Physical intimacy, copulation etcetera."

Juliette: "Oh No! He is simply a donor, we have ways of collecting the needed specimens. He is allowed to have one mate though."

Longbow: "I take back what I said."

Russell: "I assume that your science genetically engineers for only females to be born. How often do you birth a male?"

Juliette: "When need be."

Longbow: "What happens to the Architect?"

Kaira: "We don't need two. He is disposed of."

Michael: "Disposed? How?"

Juliette: "He is given a party in his honor where he is given the drink of ascension."

Longbow: "Poisoned in other words."

Kaira: "It is a mixture that puts him in a dreamlike state as he takes his last breath. At that time he ascends to the gods."

Michael: "What will the Shayan's think about human males?"

Kaira: "I am unsure. Our initial reaction is of attractiveness. You seem compatible to us."

Juliette: "We are of course a female civilization, adding men into the mix distracts some and is seen as disruptive."

Michael: "Interesting. Perhaps, when we return you to your home my wife and daughter should accompany you to Omari."

Juliette: "I think that would be best. They will be honored for the heroic deed of saving us."

Longbow with a look of disappointment at this particular news, "Will they be in any danger?"

Juliette: "No! As a gesture of appreciation they will attend a celebration that goes through the night and then return to the ship with gratitude."

Meanwhile, J is taking the thoughts of all these involved in, he sits back in a chair with a curious grin. He occasionally looks toward Rebecca's way as she nervously returns his look. Rebecca seems to have forgotten that J can read thoughts; she is having some thoughts of his well-proportioned muscular red eyed guest. J too is having similar thoughts and happy humans cannot read his mind although it doesn't take a mind reader to see a spark has ignited. Michael casually notices the twos discomfort and why, Michael grins.

Michael: "Ladies and J, Longbow will show you to some guest quarters where you can relax and refresh yourselves. We will be arriving at Shaya tomorrow evening. In the meantime please make yourselves at home." Michael then excused himself to return to the bridge.

Chapter 14

Shaya

The next evening as the Phoenix approaches Shaya, Juliette gives coordinates to Michael and was able to communicate the good news to Omari of their rescue and their homecoming.

Shaya is a planet about two thirds the size of Earth, similar in design, with sixty percent of the planet being water and the remaining lush forests. It has no frozen poles, the vegetation is maintained by a water canopy that exists over the entire planet. The constant temperature of eighty degrees Fahrenheit, and a humidity of eighty five percent.

Michael looking over to Kathy, “Don’t party too hard honey, we aren’t as young as we used to be.”

Kathy with a smirk, “I was going to get embarrassingly drunk with this first contact.”

Michael: “You will do great! It is good to have a civilization owe us one.”

Michael and Kathy prepare the Phoenix for atmospheric entry, as the Phoenix rotates for the burn all are strapped in.

Lizzy: “Burn complete captain, we are three hundred miles from target landing site. Bearing set and communicated to your comm panel.”

Michael: "Copy that! Prepare the landing party for departure." Looking at Kathy, "Have fun, but not too much."

Kathy returns his gaze, "See you in the morning."

The Phoenix traveled over a large body of water before crossing the lush landscape, she slows while firing here landing thrusters to a meadow where a delegation of Shayan's are awaiting on its perimeter. Michael lands the Phoenix gently and powers down the engines, "It's been a pleasure ladies, give our best to Omari. Hatch open, landing party you are clear for departure. Out!" At that he sat back in his seat looking out the window at what was unfolding.

Kathy and Rebecca followed Juliette and Kaira down the gang plank where small greeting party of six Shayan's were making their way across the meadow to meet them. Their greeting displayed was a one armed wrap where in our culture we go for it and use both arms for a hug. The delegation were sincerely delighted at the sight of their long lost sisters. Juliette and Kaira after the displays of affection step aside and Juliette introduces Kathy and Rebecca. The delegation similarly gives them the half hug. The group then made their way into the lush forest where Michael loses sight of them.

The ten of them walked along a path made of stone, lined with trees and low lying ferns. All the Shayan's were tall and statuesque wearing natural weaves covering their breasts and lower region exposing their mid-section while showing off their long legs. Most of them were brunettes although a few were dirty blondes. Similar features with mostly brown eyes with a few with hazel. These were fit women and would compete against most males in battle. Rebecca fit right in with her age, Kathy on the other hand was definitely the oldest on in the group. Kathy though holds her own in beauty, being tall, brunette with her blue eyes she was good competition for these young ladies in her looks and especially in her combat skills.

Making their way down the path to a clearing to a large city of about two hundred thousand. The building all made from natural resources of stone, wood and grasses laid out in a circular design the center piece looking like a Mayan pyramid, some one hundred feet high. The city is busy with foot traffic, as the ten of them make their way through the cities market place and residential areas, Juliette and Kaira were greeted over and over again by smiling faces while Kathy and Rebecca were kindly acknowledged. Nothing but beautiful women left and right as they come upon the pyramid.

The Pyramid has a beautiful entrance inlaid with gold and gems, they enter the large structure, the corridors are well light with illuminating torches, the floors are made of cut onyx stone smoothed and polished. They make their way to a brightly lit chamber where Omari is seated in the center of, a throne made for a queen with eight attendants around her. Upon Entering her chamber Omari stands up and walks over to greet Juliette and Kaira, they kneel as she draws closer along with the other Shayan's.

Omari in what seems to be her mid-thirties, long flowing auburn hair, brown eyes, high cheek bones and standing about six foot three she is a picture of beauty. She speaks holding a smile, "Rise my daughters, it is good to have you home again. Who do I owe a debt of gratitude too for delivering you safe to us?"

The Shayan's stand erect, Juliette speaks with respect, "It is the crew of the ship that brought us here, the Phoenix." Gesturing to Kathy and Rebecca, "Here is two of her crew, Kathy and her daughter Rebecca."

Omari smiles and approaches them, "It is an honor to meet a mother and daughter as the savior of my daughters. I would like to express our warmest greeting and invite you to stay the night with our people in celebration of the return of our lost ones. I want to thank you personally for your heoism."

Kathy, with a returning smile, "It is our pleasure to reunite your daughters to their family. As a mother also, we will welcome your hospitality and enjoy spending the evening getting to know your people."

Omari looking up at the attendants, claps her hands with a smile, "Prepare a festival for your sisters and our guests, we will celebrate this evening." At that command the attendants left the chambers to make the appropriate arrangements for the celebration. "Now, Kathy and Rebecca. I would like to spend some time with you. I am unfamiliar with your kind."

Kathy: "Human."

Omari: "Yes. Please join me in my chambers where we can get acquainted." Omari led the way as Juliette, Kaira and the others left to their homes and friends. Omari, Kathy and Rebecca entered a lush living space on the top level of the pyramid with panoramic views of the city, Omari gestured for them to take a seat in a deeply cushioned sofa.

Rebecca: "Thank you!"

Kathy: "Yes, thank you! This is a beautiful view of your lovely city."

Omari accepting their gratitude, "Youre very welcome. Thank you for the complement of our home. Now, tell me, are your two leaders in your world?"

Kathy: "Our planet is many lifetimes from this one. It has an equal proportion of both male and females in the population, we are simply explorers that happen to come upon your daughters being held in a prison with an associates officer. We simply did what we deem as right in delivering them safe back home."

Omari is delighted by the good nature of these humans and is at the same time intrigued that their species shares a planet with the opposite sex in such numbers.

Rebecca: "If I may."

Omari: "Go ahead child, you don't need to ask permission to speak."

Rebecca: "Our world is in need of help in several resources, the Phoenix' whole mission right now is to find those resource on a planet far from here to aid our species to continue to exist. Our planet "Earth" is in dire need for these minerals roe face certain extinction."

Omari leans over with concern and amazement that these two are on such a noble mission. "I am impressed. Normally in the void of space I come across many different species, built few and far in between do I come across a crew that is on such an unselfish mission. It follows to reason that you would help those in need when you come across them."

Kathy: "I wish all humans were like us. It is the human races short sightedness that has brought us to these desperate measures."

Omari with a query, "If you are many lifetimes from here and you are going to travel far from here, how is this possible?"

Kathy seeing that she is probing to deep and still not knowing if she could be trusted replies, "Our ship is very old and we have been in space for many years, although we can travel quickly we still have a long way to go."

Rebecca see's why her mother was stretching the truth. Omari sits back and shows a complimentary look, "You indeed should be commended. To sacrifice years to help many that perhaps won't show you the same sacrifice is above and beyond what I have seen in my life time."

Kathy see's she dodged a bullet, "Tell us, the Zurrians, why did they have two of your kind?"

Omari holding a hand to her chin in a thoughtful pose, "Despite what you see here in our capital, we do have advanced technology. Our planet defenses are among the best in the galaxy. The Zurrians had mounted a ground campaign against us by taking advantage of a mole in our society that lowered our shields briefly. She was quickly discovered after her betrayal and dealt with. That brief interruption allowed the Zurrian guard to make their way into our surrounding villages and abduct Juliette and Kaira holding them hostage for the schematics of our multiphasic shields. I do not negotiate with terrorists and especially give them a technology that will propagate their means!"

Kathy with empathy, "I am glad we came along when we did."

Omari, "I as well. You are considered a friend of the Shayans from here on out. Our home is yours." Omari then pressed a button, attendants came into the room, "Please excuse me, my position has many demands on my time, Aurora and Sheyna will make sure you are comfortable, I would suggest taking a stroll around the city, my people would love to meet you."

Kathy and Rebecca stand up, Kathy speaks with gratitude, “That would be nice. We have been cooped on our ship for a long time.”

Kathy and Rebecca exit her chambers and follow there escorts outside, Aurora with her hazel eyes asked, “It is a pleasure to escort you two. We are grateful for rescuing our sisters, what would you like to do?”

Rebecca: “I am kind of hungry, where can we go to get a small bite to eat?”

Sheyna smiles, “In the market place we have many things, I am sure you will enjoy what we have.”

Kathy smiles, “Wonderful! Lead the way.”

As the girls enjoy Shaya and its amenities, Michael is tending to J and the Phoenix.

Michael: “Russell, get a line to Primus on the Eaglefire.”

Russell: “Copy that.”

Michael: “Lizzy?”

Lizzy: “Copy.”

Michael: “Locate the Eaglefire and create an intercept course.”

Lizzy: “Tommorow launch?”

Michael: “Affirmative!”

Russell: “I have Primus on the comm for you captain.”

Michael: “Patch him through.”

Russell: “Copy.”

Michael: “Primus?”

Primus: "Copy old buddy! What’s cooking?”

Michael: “I have good news to report. J is on board and in good shape.”

Primus: “You have earned our support. I will send on all deep space comms to lay off you and your ship.”

Michael: “I appreciate that, really do.”

Primus: “Where are you now?”

Michael: “J had a couple girlfriends in jail with him, Shayan’s. We are on Shaya at the moment till tomorrow. I had to make sure the girls got home, as a gentleman.”

Primus laughing, “Yes! As a gentleman? A planet worthy to be visited over and over again if I were a young man.”

Michael laughing in return, “I don’t think my heart could take the sight of an entire planet looking like that.”

Primus: “Can I talk to my officer?”

Michael: “Of course, give me a moments.” Reaching down to the comm button, “Longbow, please escort J up to the helm.”

Longbow: “Aye, aye captain.”

Michael: "He will be here in a minute."

Primus: "Rescue? Difficult?"

Michael: "Between the vampire and spider crabs, nope! Not much. Kind of fun in hindsight." At that moment J enters the bridge.

J: "You wanted to see me captain."

Michael: "I have someone on the line that wants to talk to you."

J slipped on the comm headgear, "This is J."

Primus: "How are you son?" A smile comes across Michael's face, no wonder he cared so much about this one officer.

Michael: "I will leave you two alone for a little catching up." Michael gets up from his seat and goes to the lower levels strategy room.

Ten minutes later j knocks on the door, "Enter" Michael states.

J: "I want to thank you for all you have done to help myself and the Shayans to return to our families."

Michael: "It was nothing, but you're certainly welcome."

J: "My father wanted to express his gratitude again for your efforts."

Michael see's there is more on J's face and words, "And?"

J: "I asked my father if I could stay on board the Phoenix for a while, if that's O.K. with you?"

Michael leans back in his chair eyeing the boy up and down.

J: "I know what you're thinking…."

Michael holds up his hand, "I would appreciate it if you would let me talk after I think it, or else you and I will be holding this conversation four meters away from each other."

J: "Of course! I apologize."

Michael leaning forward with hands on the table clasped together, "I know I can't read your mind like you can read mine, but it is quite obvious that my daughter has caught your eye. Let me warn you that her singleness is by choice, I don't want to get your hopes up."

J smiles, "You forget, I can read minds."

Michael smiles, "Indeed, so she is thinking about reciprocating your feelings?"

J: "That is the initial reaction."

Leaning back in his chair folding his arms across his chest Michael in a fatherly tone, "An Elgarian and a human? My, my, my! Well son, I would advise you to take it slow. Human women need to be respected, heard and treated with dignity. Becca, is a warrior but still a woman and my daughter, don't forget that! She needs to respect you before she begins to love you."

J: “I understand.”

Michael laughs, “No, not yet but you will if your heart is set on her.”

J looks at him with a curious look thinking about what he said, he thought he understood.

Michael: “In the meantime I need to find you something to do on this ship.” Michael sat behind the table looking at J with one eyebrow up, “Got it! Intelligence officer! Having you on the ship gives us insights on this and neighboring sectors and allows me to fool the women in thinking that I thought of you staying on board.”

J smiles with approval, “Indeed, I can help the mission by my familiarity of the differing species in the realm.”

Michael smiles, “Good! Settled then, you are now my intelligence officer while we are in these sectors.”

J: “And after?”

Michael grins, “You will see if there is a future with my daughter or not by the time we finish our mission.” He motions his hand toward the door, “Now young man, get to work, we are headed to Xalon52.”

J: “Where?”

Michael: “Talk to Lizzy, she will show you.” J nods and exits the door. Sitting back in his chair with a small smile thinking, ‘An Elgarian?’ Humph!

Chapter 15

The Architect

The Festival commences on Shaya. In the cities courtyard, booths encircle they two hundred meter area, strings of lights have been hung on a star pattern over the area. Music from various percussion instruments play a rhythmic tune. Dancing in a square dance fashion is visible to the music. Kathy and Rebecca enter the courtyard with Aurora and Sheyna with smiles and a look of wonder on them. They make their way over to a tiered seating area where they see Omari and whom they would logically guess is the Architect, the only male in this society sitting to her right on the next level down from her seat.

Aurora and Sheyna, kneel upon getting close to the queen. Kathy and Rebecca bow their heads to showing submission to her authority. Omari stands and the festivities pause, everyone is on their feet including the Architect. Omari, approaches them, as she takes each step down from her perch, she smiles even greater at seeing the two humans. "Welcome!" Turning them towards the crowd and raising her voice, "We gather tonight to honor those worthy of honor. Humans from Earth!" The crowd applause, "Kathy and her daughter Rebecca along with their crew have traveled many light years to our system and unselfishly liberated two of our own!" At that moment, Juliette and Kaira stood up from the stands, the women raised their volume to show their appreciation. Omari raised one hand and it quieted, "These two and there crew are deemed as friends of the Shayan's, we will celebrate the return of our loved ones and the new friendship we have made with our hero's. Now let's go back to celebrating the end of a dark day!" The crowd immediately went back to enjoying themselves.

Omari motioned to Kathy and Rebecca to follow her up the steps and to take their seats between her and the Architect. The Architect gazed in wonderment as they made their way up to their seats, positioned between him and the queen. With a curious smile on his face, leans over and say, "Humans? Interesting, are you bioligcally compatible with Shayan's?

Rebecca feeling his gaze on her replied to that question, "Although we may be compatible, you look like you are too fragile to take on the task." As she gave him one last look before turning her attention to the festivities.

The Architect laughed and admired the humans demeanor. She is a warrior and has a confidence that one does not find every day. He leans over closer to Rebecca but this time addressing Kathy, "I would like to introduce you to my mate, Priscilla."

Priscilla leans forward to acknowledge the two, "It is an honor to meet you two. I am so grateful to you. If there is anything we can do for you please we would be happy to accommodate."

Kathy: “It is our pleasure. We simply did what was right and are happy that it turned out this way/”

The Architect smiled, “What is right? That is different. We see many come and go on Shay and in this part of space we seldom hear of any doing the right thing. Many serve themselves, the sens of right and wrong leans towards the wrong not the right."

Kathy: “That is a shame. On our planet it, all humans have an innate sense of right and wrong, it is true many choose the latter but they all know what is right.”

The Architect leans back as if he is a king addressing Rebecca again, “You know who I am?”

Rebecca rolls her eyes in her mother’s direction and then turns to him, “Yes. You are called the Architect because you donate the necessary materials for the Shayans to reproduce.”

The Architect: ”Yes, but you make it sound like an experiment. I am the father of many here. In fact the two you rescued are my daughters. Priscilla is the daughter of the Architect prior to me.”

Rebecca: “Sounds like you got your hands full.” As she smiles.

The Architect:”I have room on my agenda for a few more activities. How do the humans reproduce?”

Rebecca did not want to give this conceded individual a lesson on the birds and the beers, “Well, it is simple, the woman chooses a man and they stay with each other for life. During that lifespan the two cohabitate and produce offspring."

The Architect: "Have you chosen a man yet?"

Rebecca seeing she is not going to get out of this conversation easily, "YES!"

Kathy leans forward at this news, all the time she has enjoyed the banter and seeing her daughters discomfort in the conversation.

The Architect is curious, "Please tell me about him and where is he?"

Rebecca: "He is Elgarian, he is back on the ship. He too is a warrior and can be very jealous."

The Architect, "Elgarians, I find their mind reading annoying."

Rebecca: "I find it refreshing, I do not have to talk as much and he always knows how to make me happy."

The Architect leans forward, "And do you too have a mate?" addressing this time to Kathy.

Kathy with a small smile, "Oh yes. He too is back on the ship, is the captain and we have been together many years as you can see by looking at Rebecca."

The Architect leans back with a disappointed look, puts his arm around Priscilla and starts to enjoy the festivities. Kathy leans over to Rebecca, "An Elgarian huh?" with a smile. Rebecca nudges her mother with her shoulder and a smile.

The festivities went beyond what the girls could bear, being very tired. Omari observes that they are tired and waves an attendant over, "Kaira will take you to your quarters where you can rest. I would enjoy it if you would join me in the morning for a meal before you depart."

Kathy and Rebecca stand up, Kathy addressing Omari, "Yes, we too would enjoy that." They both followed Kaira through the festivities all the while Shayans thanked them.

Morning came all too quickly, Omari was in her dining area with a spread of fruits and delicacies fit for a queen. Kathy and Rebecca enter being led by Kaira, Kathy greets Omari, "Good morning. This looks delicious."

Omari smiles and waves her hand to invite the two to be seated. "I wanted to thank you one last time without distraction."

Kathy thanks Omari for being a gracious host. As they eat Omari continues. "You and your crew, and as I hear your crew is your family, should be commended. Where do you go from here?"

Kathy: "As you know our journey is still ahead of us with uncertainties of what we will come upon next. We must get to the resource planet and then we have to create a trade route for the materials."

Omari sees the sincerity in Kathy, "I would like to help you and your people."

Rebecca without thinking quickly states, "We need a doctor."

Omari: "Why? Is someone in need of care?"

Kathy: "No! We don't have a doctor on board, my son has been trying, but he is nothing more than a medic, some things are simply beyond hem. This request is too much to ask."

Omari gesturing to Kaira to come closer, "Go get Alala and tell her about their need so she can come here." Kaira at once exits the room to get Alala. "Alala, is my best doctor and will be a great help to you and your crew if indeed you come across any surprises."

Kathy thinking about what her husband will say when she shows up with a doctor, and one that I am sure Russell would like to train. "This isn't necessary."

Omari objects, "But it is. You can have Alala as long as you need her or as long as she wishes to stay."

The three of them eat their meal when Alala enters the room. Alala is tall with dirty blonde hair, hazel eyes, small waist and large breasts. She is tanned and her high cheek bones make her a candidate for a beauty pageant. Omari grants her permission to approach.

Alala: "Kaira tells me the newcomers need a doctor on their journey."

Omari: “Yes. Are you willing to help them?”

Alala with a smile, “Yes. It is an honor to be able to repay back to them for sving my sisters. Kaira has told me in what little time we had about their family. It would be an honor.”

Omari smiles, “There! You now have a doctor.”

Kathy: “I can’t tell you how happy I am and how grateful I am at your generosity.”

The four of them finish eating and farewells are exchanged. Alala leads the two out of the room and through the streets of the city heading back to the Phoenix.

Chapter 16

New Officers

The sun rises on Shaya with a magnificent display of reds and purples. The tree tops silhouettes are striking as Michael sits in his chair on the bridge and takes it all in. Looking out he sees Kathy and Rebecca with Alala entering the meadow, with a small smile he is guessing that he may have a surprise ahead of him. Michael makes his way down to the hatch to greet the three of them. "Good morning!"

Kathy: "Good morning."

Michael: "Who do we have here?" Reaching out his hand to welcome ALala. "I am Michael. The captain of the Phoenix."

Alala smiles and shakes his hand, "I am ALala. I am the chief doctor of Shaya. We were informed you do not have a doctor on board." Michael smiles at his wife. "I am here to help in any way I can in your journey."

Kathy holding her hand up as to ask permission to interrupt, "Honey. The Shayans wanted to help us and we thought..."

Micahel interrupting, "Welcome Alala. You are a generous and self-sacrificing woman to do this for strangers."

Alala: “The way Kaira and Juliette talk about you and your crew, it is my honor to help.”

Michael smiles and gives his wife a grin of approval and then leads the three of them into the ship. Michael looks at Rebecca, “Please show Alala her quarters and then after we launch you can introduce her to your brother.” He said with a big smile.

Michael and Kathy head up to the bridge and take their seats at the helm. Michael still with a faint smile, looking out the window and hitting some switches, “Doctor huh?”

Kathy smiling, “Thought Russell would appreciate a little help in sickbay.”

Michael Laughs, “Closing the hatch!” Hitting the comm button for an all ship broadcast, “Get ready for takeoff everybody.” After waiting a few minutes, “All clear Captain” is heard over the comm from Rebecca.

Michael and Kathy still with a faint smile, Michael said, “Let’s get out of here before our crew outgrows the ship.” Michael pulls back a lever to engage thrusters and the Phoenix rises above the tree tops, he rotates her eighty degrees and then hits the main engines, she disappeared from the sky quickly and from Shaya.

Michael busy piloting the ship entering space, without looking at Kathy, “I guess you should know, while you were away getting us a doctor, I got us an Intelligence Officer.”

Kathy grins, “J?”

Michael: "Why yes, how did you guess?" They both laugh.

Kathy: "I assume while I was away you and him had one of those talks."

Michael nodding his head, "Oh what do you mean?" pausing, "Of course I had a talk to the young man, but the wretch can read my mind. What he didn't know is that we can read his." They both laughed. "Anyway, his knowledge of this and neighboring sectors will prove useful to accomplish our mission."

Kathy grins and nods in agreement, "I agree. Hmm? Can we pick them or can we pick them?"

The Phoenix exits the stratosphere and into space, the light changes to darkness with a billion stars ahead. Michael looks at Lizzy at her panel, "Lizzy, please calculate our next jump point to Xalon52."

Lizzy with a surprised look, "I thought we were headed back to the Eaglefire?"

Michael: "Nope! J will be staying with us for a while, please find our next jump point for Xalon52."

Lizzy with a smile, "Aye Aye Captain."

Michael after twenty minutes or so hits the comm button for an all ship address, "I need all the crew in the strategy room." Michael and Kathy head down to the the lower level with Lizzy close behind. Entering the room a few are already there with the remainder arriving a minute or so behind the captain.

“Please sit down.” Michael said gesturing with his hand. “I wanted to fill all of you in on what some new news. Alala has unselfishly volunteered to be our doctor on this mission.” Russell is beaming. “And J will be staying on board as our intelligence officer.” No Rebecca is showing a slight Mona Lisa smile. “Lizzy has calculated our next jump point, it is three days out at current speed. I would take this time for the new members of our crew to familiarize your selves with the ship. Russell I need you to give a crash course to Alala of our sickbay.” Happiest day in the young mans life. “Zeeke, this will be the biggest jump we have every attempted.”

Zeeke: “She can do it Captain. I will prepare her as I always do.”

Michael: “I knew you would. J, I need you to look at our course and fill us in on what to expect.”

J: “Will do captain.”

Michael: “The rest of you please prepare for the unexpected, we are almost there, let’s focus on each task knowing the Human race is at stake, dismissed!”

They all rose from their seats and exited the room. Michael looking at Kathy, “Well honey, here we go.”

Russell enters sickbay with Alala close behind him, he is just happy Shayans can’t read minds. “Over here Alala. Have a seat.” He politely pulls the chair out for her before sitting down himself. “We have a lot of things to go over, first of all I you to get familiar with our anatomy." Noticing the possible double meaning, he stutters, "I, I mean, well, the differences between yours and mine." Thinking that didn't come out right either.

Alala seeing his awkwardness, "I know what you mean Russell."

Russell: "First let me get you out of those clothes." Blushing and still fumbling over things, "I mean into something for suitable for your assignment." Russell walks over to the closet and grabs a uniform fitted for Rebecca, "Here this should fit." Turning around he sees the tall beautiful Alala removing her top exposing her large breasts, perfect in every way. Russell blushing and trying not to break the horizon but delighted to no end hands her the uniform. "Alala?"

"Yes." Alala responded as she removes her lower garment, Russell seeing that the Shayan's are compatible to human men.

"Personally I do not mind you dressing in front of me, but on earth and in our culture a person dresses in private out of the view of others." Russell said as straight face as he could.

Alala slips into the blue uniform, pulling it down over her waist as her breasts bigger than Rebeccas try to push out of the v neck and her bottom fills the suit just perfectly. "There!" She says, "How does it look?" Wrong guy to ask.

"You look great!" Russell smiled

Alala: "I will try to remember not to dress in front of others in the future except for you since you don't mind it."

Russell smiled, "Good! I mean good." He then gave Alala a tour of the facility before asking her to get on the examination table for a body scan. "We need to scan your anatomy so the computer can make suggestions in case you are injured." Alala hops onto the table and lays down. "This will not hurt at all but will take a little while as your anatomy gets recorded."

Alala takes a deep breath pushing her breasts to the breaking point in that outfit, Russell is doing all he can to stay professional. Russell then moves the scanner over her head and presses a few buttons, "Try to stay perfectly still during this process, take a nap. I will wake you when it is done." The tall statuesque beauty closed her hazel eyes and started to sleep. Russell was thanking his parents over and over again in his mind.

Rebecca, Longbow and J are in the strategy room going over the course, J sees a lot he needs to talk to the captain about. "Call your father down here." J asks Rebecca.

"What is wrong?" Rebecca asked.

J was insistent, "Please Becca ask him to come down here, I need to fill him in on that sector."

Rebecca summons her father and enters the room minutes later, "What's going on?" Michael asked.

J replied, “We have a lot to go over. You want the good news first or the bad news?”

Michael with a worried look on his said, “The bad news and then cheer me up with the good.”

J goes to the screen on the wall displaying a star map of the sector they ae about to jump into, “Here we go! These coordinates we are jumping to is smack dab in the middle of a civil war.”

Longbow: “Bloody Hell!”

J continues, “This war is different from other civil wars. It is a proxy war.”

Michael with a concern look, “Proxy for who?”

J continues, “Hegelians. Hegel decades ago lost their king in death. His twin sons became the co rulers of the planet, these princes at first did well but in time they grew board and came up with a live game of strategy using two very different worlds in their solar system, Klio and Quino.”

Michael: “These two spoiled brats are playing a live game of chess?”

J: “Yes! They could not have picked two better opponents, these two by nature natural enemies. The though did not have the means to fight each other or space travel. The Hegelian Princes equipped and trained the two worlds to fight and thus a never ending game began. We are about to enter the game board when we jump.”

The three of them are disgusted at this news and concerned. Michael asked "What's the good news?"

J: "The planet you call Xalon52 is really called Bontha, The Bonthas are easy to trade with."

Michael: "Well that is good news. Let's get to talking about this chess match." Pausing and sitting back in his chair with his arms folded, "We need to stop this war. We cannot create a trade route through a warzone." Michael gives out a big sigh, "J, Rebecca and Longbow, you will stay here and come up with a plan to stop those blue blooded brats from continuing this game." Shaking his head he gets up, "Please report back to me when you have a plan."

With Longbow, J and Rebecca in the room, Rebecca asked a lingering question, "What do you mean by a perfect pick for the princes?"

J: "The two worlds have very different civilizations. Klio's inhabitants are reptilian based sentient beings and Quino's inhabitants are Insect like creatures."

Longbow: "Sounds like lizards eating fly's."

J: "Yes. Both stood alone happy in their eco systems until Hegel interrupted their life course."

Longbow: "How do we stop these two from doing what comes naturally?"

J: "We could just kill the princes."

Rebecca: "No! I don't think we have to go that far." Looking at J, "You need to call your father. With the power of the Yag Coalition we can threaten these two to the point of submission."

J: "And if they don't listen to the threat?"

Longbow: "Then we kill one of them, shooters choice." He said with a grin.

J continues to brief the team on the planet Hegel and where the two princes live.

Chapter 17

WAR by Proxy

Tow days later everyone is gathered in the strategy room, Michael addresses them, "This will be an interesting jump for all of us, Zeeke? Is th Phoenix prepared for the jump of this distance?"

Zeeke: "Yes Captain."

"That is good." Michael continues, "We will be jumping into hostile territory, a war that is being fought between two worlds for the pleasure of another. This is disgusting to each and every one of us. It is morally irreprehensible and must be stopped. First we need to stop it because it is wrong and second we cannot create a trade route through a warzone.

"J has contacted Primus of the Yag Coalition, we will be using the mighty muscle of the Yag to persuade these two princes to cause a cease fire. They will recall all instruments of war and rebuild the worlds they have selfishly disrupted."

Russell:"What if they won't do it?"

"Well, we aren't giving them much of a choice." Michael continues, "If need be, and I don't think it will be needed, one of the princes will be killed to persuade the other. As our intel informs us, these two are cowards and should back down as soon as we propose this option."

Alala: "What is the plan to meet them?"

Michael: "I am glad you asked. First we will ask poloitely."

Alala: "Secondly?"

Michael smiles, "Secondly, we will go in and storm their castle. The away team will be J, Rebecca, Longbow and I. The rest of you willstay on the ship as I am sure they will send interceptors after the Phoenix. You will be signaled when we have accomplished the mission to come and pick us up." Looking at Alala, "I am glad you are on board, between the away team and the team on the Phoenix, I expect some cuts and bruises, or worse."

Alala: "Sickbay will be ready to receive any injured."

"I hope we come out unscathed." Michael continues, "This will be a dicey mission, all of us need to be prepared for anything and everything." All at the table are silent contemplating how to execute their tasks. "Is there any questions?" All are silent, "Then good! We warp in thirty minutes, let's all get to our stations." They all get up in urgency with serious looks on all their faces." Michael looks at Kathy with a grin, "Well? This will be fun." She smiled back.

Everyone is at their stations ready for the warp jump, Michael gives the command, "Zeeke, initiate the warp drive." The warp drive comes online and powers the front and rear emitters, space begins to bend, stretch and pull around them as the stars distort and then in a moment the old starry sky is replaced with a new one. Michael calls to Lizzy, "Lizzy, what is the status of where we landed?"

Lizzy: "Looks clear for now." Gazing at her screen even more and widening out its coverage, "Wait! I see two distinct groupings not far from here, yes........there they are. The Klio's and the Quin's are fighting about seven thousand kilometers from us."

Michael: "Chart a path around the battle and take us to Hegel, we have a war to stop." Anger on his face at this whole situation.

Lizzy: "Aye captain!"

The Phoenix makes her way around the battlefield and comes upon Hegel, a planet about two thirds the size of earth with rings like Saturn. Blueish green with the rings in shades of blue, it is a beautiful addition to this solar system. Michael hits the comm for an outside channel, "Hegel, this is the Phoenix, request permission to land at the castle." Silence on the radio so Michael repeats himself and waits.

"What is your business here?" A voice sternly asked.

Michael: "We have an urgent matter to discuss with the princes, it is life or death in importance." Meaning their life or death.

"You are not welcomed here, permission denied!"

Michael: "Who is it that denies us permission to land?"

"I am general Syed of the royal guard. I said denied and that is the final word, now leave our territory or feel our punishment."

The radio went silent, Michael looking at Kathy, "Well, plan B it is then." Becca, Longbow and J, get ready at the hatch and fetch my gear I will meet you there when we land. We will have to exit quickly so the Phoenix can lead them away."

At that moment Lizzy interrupts, "Dad! Ihave three inbound bogies launched from the surface. They will enter space in ninety seconds."

Michael: "Copy that! We will start the burn at the moment they hit the stratosphere buying us a little more time. They will have to turn and start a burn to follow. Lizzy! Countdown our entry to Hegel. We need to pass them relatively close."

Lizzy: "Aye Captain! Get ready." A few seconds tick off the clock, all of them have adrenalin pumping through their bodies, then," six, five, four, three, two, NOW!"

Michael pushes the Phoenix into the atmosphere, fire engulfing the ships hull, she breaks through the clouds with a loud boom. Racing over the planets landscape, Michael slows it down as much as he dares to navigate through thou tall peaks and valleys of a mountainous terrain, looking at Kathy "Here you go honey, sh is all yours."

Kathy accepts a peck on the forehead, “Don’t get hurt!”

Michael smiles, “Top of the agenda!” Then makes his way to the exit hatch to suit up.

The Phoenix slows down and rotates to descend on a ledge about two kilometers from the castle which is situated on the peak. Kathy fires the landing thrusters simultaneously opening the hatch, as soon as the Phoenix touches the ground the away team exit, the Phoenix lifts off closing the hatch and rotating itself to resume the last course. The away team runs to cover in tall vegetation.

Chapter 18

Castle Assault

Hegel is a lush and colorful planet, with no frozen poles land sits between the oceans and the thick clouds above. The clouds offer a humidity that waters the fauna on the ground. It never rains on this planet but it feels like it through your seat glands. Michael surveys the topography, "J you will lead the way while Longbow and eye cover your three and nine, Rebecca you cover our six.

Wildlife is heard through the grasses and tall trees with a widespread canopy litter the landscape. The team looks to the sky to see if any aerial surveillance is active for which there is none. The team, eyes the castle up ahead. The castle is built into and sits on top of the peak of this mountain, it has round watchtowers that are huge obviously providing rooms and space for the castle. There two center columns, one larger and taller than the other, which is the main home for the princes. The top of the tallest column sits a structure like a house with gardens and fountains. That is the princes residence. The team must make it past the double fortified walls of the castle and gain entry to one of the towers and make their way to the top of the tallest one.

Around the castle there is a foot path leading to several entrances, the team make their way around to a secondary entrance and wait. Two sentries are headed their way, J makes a motion in silence that there are two of them and for Rebecca and Longbow to circle around them to subdue them. Rebecca and Longbow understand and silently leave Michael and J. Michael and J stay concealed in the brush as the guard's come closer, J motions to Michael to stay quiet and that they are almost upon them. Rebecca and Longbow without making a sound come up behind the two unsuspecting guard's and simultaneously wrapped one arm around their neck to choke and the over hand over their mouths to silence them. In less than ten seconds the men were unconscious and on the ground. Michael and J quickly helped Rebecca and Longbow drag the men into the brush. Michael searched their pockets for an access key and came to know surprise one had one. The team tied them up and gagged them.

The team made it to a lesser entrance of the castle, Michael used the the access card and the door opened with J first and each of them resuming their coverage, the door closed behind them as they entered a tunnel leading to the grounds in front of the second wall. J surveys any sentries about hiding in the shadow of the tunnel, visible, one sentry looking at the tunnel where they are, J hand motions that one is elevated and looking at where they are. Rebecca comes forward to take point, pulling out a small throwing knife, she steps beyond the shadow of the tunnel, the guard is stunned at the presence of an alien and grabs his horn to sound the alarm, Becca takes the knife and hurls it.

The knife lands with pin point accuracy in his juggler, muting him as he falls from his perch.

Rebecca looks back at her father, gives a shrug then J leads them to the base of that wall. These walls are towering above them some thirty feet made of brick and stone they are some fourteen feet thick. There is no coverage to hide behind as they make it to the door of the second wall, J grabs a knife from his belt and Hurls it to the chest of another guard who spotted them from his perch on the first wall. J gives a glance at Rebecca like he was keeping score. Michael uses the key to open the door of the second wall, they file into the tunnel closing the door behind them.

This tunnel leads to a courtyard for what looks like an open air market. Hegelians are milling about, going about their normal lives. This will be difficult to blend in since Hegelians short in stature. Michael looks at all the booths and the timing of traffic, trying to come up with a plan to cross the marketplace and gain entry into the closest tower.

Michael and the team are surveying the situation; there is a garment booth not far from the entrance to the tunnel, if only they could get close enough. J is the most capable since he can see movements through mind reading, he can be one step ahead of the crowd. J crouches down to lower himself about a foot, he enters the crowd, from where the team is it looks like he will be seen but every move he makes he avoids detection till finally he is by the booth. J grabs four garments, puts one on and heads toward the tunnel.

The team are impressed at his avoidance of detection. Each member dons a garment and bows low to enter the walkway. The marketplace foot traffic picks up as the go deeper, with their heads bowed down so their faces are not discernable they make way to the first tower.

Entering the tower they discard the garments and make their way up the staircase. As it winds up the perimeter of the round tower, two forward and two their six as they make their way up the four foot wide staircase. There would be no escaping any traffic in this situation. Two guard's head them off and are startled at the discovery of these aliens, Michael and J rush them, J easily subdues his opponent while Michael throws a punch to the sternum and then punches the throat, the guard doubles over as he brings his nee up into his face rendering his guard unconscious.

Stepping over the men, the team makes their way up the staircase until a loud alarm is sounded. One of the casualties must have been discovered, their pace quickens until they get to the opening of the foot bridge leading to the center and most prominent tower where the princes reside. Running across the bridge sentries on the roof top spot them and release a round of fire, Rebecca and Longbow return the fire striking two of the guard's causing them to fall from their perch. Upon entering the center tower, Becca looks at J and holds up two fingers to his two. J returns the gesture with a smug look.

Michael and J lead the other two up the staircase where guard's are descending and ascending the stairs to cut them off, with only four feet of room the four of them create space so they can engage the pursuers. Rebecca throws a series of punches and kicks before pulling out a two edge knife and begins to drive it into her attacker, yelling "THREE!" as she takes on another.

J hearing the number steps up to the plate and takes on two attackers, using his alien strength each punch he throws has the impact of a hammer causing the attackers to fall as he delivers one last blow to each yelling "Three AND Four!"

Michael and Longbow find the yelling of numbers oddly entertaining as they fight their attackers hitting their faces, sternum and then chins, Michael yells out "Twenty One!" as Longbow smiles.

Rebecca knocks another and slashes another yelling out "Four AND Five!" then looking at her father, "Twenty one huh!" he smiled back as more guard's came. One after another as they worked their way up the stairs fell to the sounds of J and Rebecca yelling out numbers in a tight race. The descending guard's stopped and allowed the team to make way to the top, running down the hallway to a grand door, Rebecca and Longbow pinning the ascending guard's with laser fire, J sets the charge on the door and blows it to smithereens. Rebecca and Longbow enter behind Michael and J while keeping the guard's at bay with laser fire, Michael enters the room where a large figure comes into view, Michael addresses him "General Syed I presume."

Syed: "Why do you assault our people and storm our home?"

"I asked politely earlier but you said no." saying it sarcastically.

Syed indignant at the sarcasm, "State your business here!"

Michael seeing the two princes cowering behind the chairs, "I assume you two are listening so I will go ahead." Looking Syed straight in the eyes, "We are humans from Earth and have heard of the crimes these two are committing for their own selfish pleasures."

Syed raises his voice in defiance, "What crimes are you speaking of and who are you to question anything we do!"

Michael speaks over the laser fire pointed down the hall, "First things first, the crime is the strategy game these two spoiled little brats are playing between Klio and Quin. Lives are being lost for what? For their amusement? This is an atrocity of great proportions and must cease at once!"

Syed angry, "Who do you think you are?"

"Oh! Sorry about that, forgot to answer that one." Saying it in a sarcastic polite manner, "We are part of the Yag Coalition of armies, our counsel has deemed that this has gone on long enough."

The face of the General starts to soften, "Why would the Yag be interested in our affairs?"

"Part of their coalition will be trading in this part of the sector and refuses to ship through a warzone so this must stop immediately!" Michael warns, "If you do not cease this war as of today, the Yag will come here and claim this planet as their own and kill any in line to rise as a leader."

Syed softens even more, "What are the terms of this ceasefire?"

"Well spoken" Michael answers, "The terms are pretty lopsided against you, you first must take away all implements of war you have supplied to those two worlds, then you must rebuild each civilization while admitting your roll in their war. Finally, you will give them whatever resources they need for the same period of time that you have had them engaged in their conflict. Those are the terms, do you agree to such terms?"

General Syed motions for the princes to come out from hiding, "We agree." With his head bowed low.

"Oh one more thing, call off your guard's, we would hate to kill anymore." Michael said with a half-smile.

Syed pulls out a comm device and presses a button to signal an all clear.

Michael: “At ease team, there won’t be any more problems.” Reaching down to his comm signals the Pheonix to arrive at the Castle courtyard.

Chapter 19

Chasing the Phoenix

The Phoenix lifts off from the bluff leaving the away team on the ground running for cover, Kathy shuts the hatch turns the phoenix and hits the thrusters reclaiming the course they just had.

Lizzy: “The bogies have reentered the atmosphere and are on an intercept course in ninety seconds.”

Kathy needs to lead them far from the castle, heading into space. “We will use the rings to throw rocks at them.” The rings of Hegel are comprised of small particles from micrometer to meters in size mostly of ice they do contain rock and ore. The rings glow in shades of blue adding beauty to this wretched planet. Kathy heads toward the inner ring, Lizzy calls out, “Three interceptors almost in firing range.”

Kathy adds more power to the front deflector array as she enters the rings. The Phoenix pushes through them spreading them apart and creating a wake behind her, the interceptors enter the wake as they are pelted with the debris they start to fly irregularly. The interceptors are a “V” shape design with two pilots the wings collapse for better aerodynamics in atmosphere. Kathy rolls the Phoenix and adjusts course radically to the left, “Charge impulse beams!” Russell already on it, “Copy and ready.”

Kathy yells, “FIRE!” Russell releases a short sustained yellow beam that hits and shears the leading interceptor disabling it in space, the two remaining ones break off their formation, one goes left and the other right trying to outflank the Phoenix. Kathy noticing this maneuver pulls the phoenix vertical rotating it while pushing the nose back down to do a horse shoe maneuver coming to the rear of one of the fighters, "FIRE!" Russell releases another energy beam destroying the second one. The third interceptor made its way to the rear of the Phoenix during that last clever move by Kathy, the interceptor releases a fury of weapon fire hitting the Phoenix dead center causing the ship to lurch and the navigation panel to explode and erupt in fire causing Lizzy to fall back hitting the floor unconscious. Russell rushes to his sisters side and radios Alala, “Sickbay we have a medical emergency, we need you here NOW!” as he yells.

Kathy unable to see what the commotion is and hoping her little girl will be fine focuses on the enemy fighter that continues to fire upon the Phoenix. Alala arrives in under a minute and tells Russell to extinguish the fire and get back to his controls. Russell presses a button and the fire goes out, furious that his little sister is hurt he returns to the weapon controls readying it to fire. Alala picks up Lizzy and carries her back to sickbay.

Kathy with adrenalin pumping and anger in her voice, “Get ready!” Russell doesn’t need to be told. His fingers on the fire buttons, Kathy pivots the ship on axis through the acceleration causing it to about face while traveling in the same direction, she yells, “FIRE!” Russell releases a volley of energy beams disintegrating the interceptor to nothing.

Kathy pulls back on a lever to halt the backward momentum of the ship, “Go check on your sister.”

Russell, “Aye, Aye!”

Kathy looks down at the control panel seeing a few warning indicators to survey the damage the Phoenix has taken

Russell rushes down to sickbay to check on Lizzy, upon entering he sees Lizzy laying unconscious on the examination table with the scanner going to and fro over her body. He rushes to her side and looks at Alala, “Well?”

Alala with a look of consolation and reassurance, “She will be fine, no broken bones and only minor burns. I am sure she will wake up soon.”

Russells face relaxes as he grabs her left hand to hold. “Thank you Alala! Thank You!”

Alala smiles seeing the love this family and their bond; almost as if they were one.

An hour later, Kathy gets the signal to come pick up the away team. Still fuming from the damage to her little girl and the ship she will not be bringing in the Phoenix without a little display of her might.

Michael and the away team make their way down to the courtyard with hundreds of Hegelians backing off of them as if they had leprosy, they see the Phoenix coming through the sky, she overshoots the castle with a sonic boom, buzzing the tower before turning around and lowering her large fuselage into the courtyard. The hatch opens as the Hegelians observe from a safe distance, the hatch closes and the Phoenix lifts off suddenly using more of her thrusters than usual causing sand and debris to kick up. The Phoenix then points toward the heavens and disappears.

Michael upon hearing about Lizzy made his way straight to sickbay with Rebecca right behind him. The two of them rushed in to the room, Lizzy was sitting up and Alala was standing next to her. Michael approaches his little girl, "How are you?"

Lizzy smiled at her father's concern, "I am fine dad, Alala patched me up and I was just about to go to my room."

Rebecca approached Alala and hugged her, "Thank you so much!"

Alala, taken by surprise by the gesture, smiled, "She didn't take too much damage."

Michael looks at her, "We appreciate for what you did. Thank you!"

Lizzy, "How did the castle look? Disneyesque?"

Michael and Rebecca smiled at her query, "It's a little messier right now than when we arrived." Michael smiled as he replied to her. Giving her a wink. "Rebecca, would you help your sister to her room for some rest?"

Lizzy, "Dad, I don't need help." Michael gives his daughter his look, "Well o.k. this time, come on sis."

Alala admires the familial environment she is in and admires the way the father cares so deeply for his children, this is a foreign thing for her to see. On her planet, the Architect cares very little about his daughters. He has limited time if any to spend with them, this, this is so different and pleasant.

Michael gives Alala a smile and then leaves the room heading for the bridge. Kathy gets up from her chair to greet her husband with a hug and a kiss, "Did you see Lizzy?" She asked.

"Yes." Michael responds with a comforting tone, "Getting a doctor was a pretty smart move. She did a great job patching her up. Becca is with her in her room. It looks like you scratched my new paint job."

Kathy rolled her eyes, "Nothing Zeeke can't fix."

Michael looking at two legs sticking out of the navigation floor panel, smiled,"Zeeke! Get some rest you old goat." Zeeke mumbles from inside the panel, Michael smiles, "Well, we are heading off to bed, make your way to yours as soon as you can" mumbling is heard again before they exit the bridge.

Chapter 20

Road to Bontha

The morning came way too early for some of the crew as the Phoenix traveled through space making its way to the target destination, Bontha. Alala got up early and made her way up to the galley where she found J sitting enjoying a light breakfast. She made her way over to the pantry, grabbed a pastry and then poured herself a cup of coffee. Sitting down next to J, they looked at each other and smiled.

J: “I know!”

Alala purses her lips, “I wish you can restrain from doing that.”

J realizing what he did, “I am sorry. Sometimes I hear the thoughts like words.”

Alala looking at J, “Different aren’t they?”

“Yes.” Giving Alala a small smile he continues, “It is a nice difference, isn’t it?”

Alala: “I have never experienced this environment of love and family. Their bond is tighter than any I have ever experienced.”

J concedes the point, "I agree. Michael leads as captain but it is so much more than that, he, well, he..."

"He is a father!" She finishes his thought. "On my planet we don't have that. It is a welcomed experience for me."

J: "I come from a military family, although I respect and love my father, he was always working. This family lives and works together, this has strengthened their bonds to one another."

Alala: "I agree. Lizzy is a genius."

J: "Rebecca too is smart and a warrior."

Alala smiles at her next remark, "Russell is quite the young man. Smart and compassionate. He does blush a lot when I am around."

J laughs, "I am sure you make several men blush. No secret, he is taken with you."

Now Alala is blushing, "And you? No secret that Rebecca has turned your head."

J sits back in his chair taking a sip of coffee, "Yes, yes I do like her. Look at us!"

Alala smiles sipping her coffee, "Yes, just look at how we are falling for this family."

J gets a serious look about him, "I wonder if....."

"We could stay?" Alala finishes his sentence.

J smiles, “Are you sure you can’t read minds. You have finished two of my thoughts.”

Alala grins, “On this topic our minds are easy to read. I have never thought about leaving Shaya. It is a scary thought, but this family comforts me and subdues my fears.”

J gives a smirk, “Me too. My father and Michael are acquaintances and have fought together, so I am sure my father would be honored to have me serve aboard the Phoenix.”

Alala contemplates what Omari would think, “My queen was very eager to help this crew after you all saved two of my sisters. When I left she gave me a goodbye look, different than a see you later look. I wonder if she knew I was going to feel this way?”

They both sat at the table finishing their breakfast and grinning at each other. Yes! These two additions to the Phoenix are making their mind up about their futures.

The all ship address summoned all crew to the strategy room. Alala and J get up and make their way to the meeting where the rest of the crew is gathering. Michael stood at the head of the table, “We have a lot to go over before landing on Bontha, Russell!” Russell alertly looks at his father, “You need to put together a proposal for what earth needs and what we can give Bontha for it. J!” J looking at Michael, “You need to verse me on the Bontha protocols so I don’t screw up by accidently offending them.” Michael looks at the entire crew, “We have come a long way, have encountered many obstacles, this is where we make it all worth it! Earth will grind to a halt if we fail, we will not fail! I have faith in each and every one of you. The away team will consist of myself, Russell, j and Rebecca. J you are coming along to give me an advantage in negotiations. Becca, you just in case and Russell who better to talk about the elements we need for earth. Any questions?" They were silent, "Good! Let's get prepared."

They all got up with J and Rebecca staying, Russell went to his station and started to work on his proposal. Michael looking at J, "Well? Keep me from making me looking like a monkeys uncle."

J had no idea what a monkey was or even what his uncle had to do with anything, but he knew what he had to say, "The Bonthas are a subterranean species, their villages and the few cities are built underground in caverns beyond the imagination. It is like a world in the middle of a world. They farm a fungi that grows despite natural light by the humidity of the thermals in these caverns. They are a mining species and as usual already know, asexual, so if they live with anyone it is because they are close friends.

"You will experience the added weight of increased gravity, but that is good."

Rebecca asks, "Why is that good?"

J answers, "Because the Bonthas don't like it when dealing with customers that move too quickly. Our movements must be slow about half of our normal speed in order to make them feel comfortable. Our speech must be simplified as well. We need to refrain from using words beyond two syllables.

"When greeting them the correct phrase is, 'You ggood!'. Because they have three arms, eyes and legs, the dominate eye is the center along with the arms. Shake the center arm while looking in the center eye. This shows a sign of respect and will set a good ton for the negotiations."

Michael carefully listening to all that J is saying asked, "What about the landing facilities and access to Barabas and Almister."

J continues, "The port is like many with a main tower and tunnels that connect the landing pads to the tower. At the base of the tower is an elevator that will take us down to the capital some one thousand meters below the surface."

While the briefing continues in the strategy room Russell is at his station preparing the proposal for the elements needed for earth. The first element is Lanthanum, this element is a rare earth element used in batteries. The technology on earth has left internal combustion behind decades ago and has adopted a battery equipped mode of transportation. Batteries to are used in everyday life including powering homes and buildings, without Lanthanum the earth would grind to a halt.

The next element is Neodymium. This element is used in magnets and magnets are critical to produce power for the world, on and off the grid. Neodymium is nearly exhausted and with out it, the power stations will grind to a halt in the near future.

The third and last is antimatter. Antimatter is nearly gone and is metal for space travel. The Phoenix uses this fuel although the stock of iridium is a parent element of antimatter it too is in short supply. Ir8dium when super heated by a laser can produce anti-protons which is antimatter.

These three elements are what the Pheonix must arrange for with the Bonthas.

Chapter 21

Bontha

The next day the teams continue to get ready for their meeting with the Bonthas. Lizzy is back at work making sure all course corrections are made to arrive at their destination. ETA to Bontha is twenty two hours two minutes and thirty two seconds.

Kathy heads down to the rec room where she finds Alala relaxing in one of the recliners. She approaches her and takes the chair next to her. “Good afternoon!” Kathy greeted her.

Alala opens her eyes and sits up, “Hello, must have dosed off for a moment. These chairs are very comfortable.“

Kathy smiles and acknowledges the remark, “That’s why we had these installed, simple old style comfort in the new age. So! How are you doing?”

Alala enjoys Kathy’s company and smiled at her, “Surprisingly well. You and Michael should be proud of your selves at how incredible your children are.”

Kathy smiles, “They are pretty impressive. Though you haven’t seen them argue yet.”

Alala grins, “Siblings can have their moments I guess.”

Kathy looks at Alala, "How are you doing? Being away from home and all, any homesickness?"

Alala: "I did at first, but as I have come to know all of you, your family has, well, made me feel as I belong here."

Kathy leans forward and grabs Alala's hand, "You do belong here. We are a family on the Phoenix, we care for each other because of the respect and yes, love we have for each other. You and J although new to our family, you have been adopted as it were into our group. We are all happy to have you." Pausing and looking Alala square in the eyes, "And would be happy to have you longer if you wished it."

Alala is warmed inside at the gesture and feels a sense of belonging. "I am glad you feel that way. Really." The two women lean back into the recliners and smile, "These really are comfortable!" Alala repeated.

In the strategy room J is practicing with Michael on his speech and his movements. "AH! I can't help it, limiting myself to two syllables is like hand cuffing an Italian." Michael exclaims. J had no idea what that meant, but was sure it stressed the difficulty of using one and two syllable words in conversation.

J reassuringly addresses Michael, "Captain, you almost have it down, you only slip once or twice. The gravity increase on the planet will naturally slow your body movements and that will remind you to simplify your speech."

“Where is Russell? Doesn’t he need to practice?” Michael in frustration asked.

J smiled, “Two syllables came a little more naturally to him. He kind of liked the simplification in speech.”

“Kids!” Michael mumbled, “OK. Let’s get on with it.”

Michael and J continued to rehearse as the ship is landing in the morning.

Bontha is a red giant planet about the size of Jupiter in Earths solar system, it is the eighth planet from the sun which is ten times larger than that of Earths Sun. The landscape on Bontha is devoid of trees and vegetation, it is rocky with tall outcroppings of stone pillars. The oceans are crimson in color with tides in excess of twenty feet, dark and looming the water is. The surface water is poison and washes the surface with an acid that steams on the shores.

The trading port where the Phoenix will be landing has several terminals to accommodate many ships at a time since trade is the way the Bonthas make their living.

Michael takes the helm in the morning and ready the team and his ship to enter the atmosphere of Bontha. “All crew! This is the captain, we are about to enter the stratosphere of Bontha and will be landing shortly, away team prepare for your mission. Out!”

Michael turns the Phoenix to an orientation of thirty degrees elevation and lowers her belly into the ionosphere causing it to flame and shake, within moments the Phoenix breaks through into the red sky and shoots over the oceans like a dart looking for its target. The scene on Bontha is desolate, no life whatsoever that is visible. The Phoenix slows as it travels over the steaming beaches and over the rocky landscape. Ahead the trading port, the tower is magnificent jetting up over two hundred feet, shining like it was made out of crystal, it is a sight to behold.

Kathy, "Captain, we have permission to land at pad twenty one."

"Copy" Michael responding while flying the Phoenix. The tower has many terminals and several other ships of very different designs, one Michael thought was really cool was a spherical ship. "Firing thrusters, prepare for touch down." Michael fires the landing thrusters and turns the ship as she comes to a soft and gentle rest on the polished stone landing pad.

Michael looking at Kathy takes a deep breath, then stands up leans over and kisses her on the forehead, "Wish me luck, stupid two syllables!" Kathy smiles and gives him a reassuring look. Michael leaves the bridge and meets Rebecca, J and Russell at the exit hatch. Russell is as giddy as a school girl. This is the mission he has been preparing for, all his work and now it is at hand. His excitement gives him a spring in his step, Rebecca and J smile over his enthusiasm.

Michael grabs his bag, looking at the three of them with Russell almost bouncing in one place, "This is it team, let's put our mouths where our money is." Michael hits the hatch button and the door opens to the red planet. Making their way in the open about fifteen meters their feet feel as if lead weights have been added to their shoes, each step is hard to lift and they fall harder thus having to use muscles to land each step. Russell on the other hand seemed to be unaffected by the added gravity. The tunnel they entered is strangely lit, with two rows of lights on the floor left and right of the walkway the cylindrical tunnel was smooth like glass but was a crystal. It is like walking through quartz crystal, the ceiling was illuminated with a warm yellow glow as if the crystal itself was illuminating. Really a beautiful display of materials.

Arriving at the end of the tunnel, it opens up to a large circular room about fifty meters in diameter. The floor has a double door hatch that looks like when opened something would arrive through it. There are iridescent lines on the floor that pertain to a clearance area we must allow for the elevators arrival. J motions for the team to wait here.

Russell with wide eyes, "You have to hand it to these Bonthas, they know how to build an airport!"

They all smile and agree, it is something to behold. The ground starts to tremor, the doors on the floor break their seal and open downward, a moment later the elevator rises slowly. The elevator is just as impressive as the tower and the terminal tunnels, it is spherical in shape with windows dispersed around its curvature, it shines like polished platinum with two doors at opposing sides of the sphere. One of the doors open, a Bontha steps out followed by two Sekorans, Sekorans planet is Sekora, they are about two feet tall but are about four feet wide, yellow and green in color they walk on four feet and have two arms. They too are traders in a neighboring sector. The Bontha gives them a farewell and then looks in the team's direction, motioning for them to approach.

Michael steps up slowly to the operator, looked him squarely in the center eye, "You good!" then reaches out to shake the center hand. The Bontha is pleased and invites the team into the elevator with another hand. When all are in, the Bontha enters and turns to a control panel about the size of a notebook tablet and enters some commands. The elevator starts to descend slowly. As they descend the elevator picks up speed, it accelerates faster and faster till the added gravitational pull is diminished and they nearly achieve zero gravity, near weightless the elevator hurls itself through the crust of Bontha till it starts to slow, gravity is again felt, even more pronounced contrasted with the weightlessness they just came from. Everyone is trying to keep from vomiting from their ride.

Out the windows they can see the capital city, magnificent! Stalagmites and stalactites with spherical buildings one next to the other and even stacked on top of each other, all are built out of the same substance the elevator is, crystals illuminate the massive cavern. Green fields are visible, evidently the fungi they grow and harvest for food. A bat like flying creature is seen flocking over the buildings changing direction in a tight formation, absolutely marvelous. Michael and J have to admit this is one of the most unique worlds one could visit.

The elevator slows to a stop and the rear door opens, the Bontha exits the elevator motioning the team to follow. Michael thanks the operator and leads the team to the commerce building. J taps michael on the shoulder, "Captain the commerce building is this way." Pointing in the opposite direction.

Michael smiles, "I knew that!" not really, "I just wanted to see this, um, thing. OK. Now I have seen it. J you can lead the way." Rebecca releases a low laugh as Michael pretends to not hear it. Russell is still light in the loafers over this away mission. The team moves slowly through the village, many hundreds of Bonthas are busy doing what Bonthas do. They arrive at a central dome, J leads the team inside.

J looking at Michael, "Here is the commerce building. You sir, will ask to see the minister of trade at that desk."

"Wait! How do I say minister and stay at two syllables? " Michael asks sarcasticly.

J grins, "Use the term trade office, we would need entry."

Michael returns his grin, "You have all the answers I guess." Rebecca smiled at the interchange and winks at J.

Michael approached the desk where a Bontha was busy writing on two different pads with two of his arms, Michael stood in front of him still and silent. The Bontha looked up, “You good!” he said.

Michael greeted him as well, “You good! I would like to meet with the trade office.”

The Bontha looks down at the screen, “Species?”

Michael answered, “Human.”

“Planet?” He asked.

“Earth.” Answering his question.

“Buy or sell?” He asked.

“Buy.” Michael replied

The Bontha looks down at his manifest and sees that earth is a new trader and is pleased at the sight of a new customer. He looks up at Michael, “You may pass, level three, door three.”

Michael thanked the clerk and made his way to the team. “level three, door three, let’s go.” The team proceeded slowly to the central elevator to go to the third floor, once there they walked down a perimeter hall way curving with the buildings shape to door three. Taking a deep breath they enter.

Almister was seated at his desk, two screens were left and right of him, a hand was typing away on his left and on his right. He stopped and stood up to greet the new customers, “You good!” he enthusiastically greeted them.

Michael: “You good!”

Almister: “Humans from Earth? New to us are you?”

Michael in a gracious manner, “Yes, we have come from a great distance to trade with you. Your reputation spans many light years all the way to our planet.”

Almister is flattered and pleased at this news, “How can we help you?”

michael puts his hand out for Russell to give him the folder, handing the folder to him, “We have need of these three things.” Michael hands the folder to Almister.

Almister studies the request, Russell even put trade options in the proposal for him to consider. J is reading his thought and understands that Almister is pleased with the terms but wants to see if he can get better terms. “Impressed I am at this folder. Who did this?” Russell stepped forward, “I did.”

Almister surveys the young man, “You did well. These things we have. I would like to talk about price.”

Russell knows he made a fair offer in the proposal, “What is wrong with the price I put down?” Russell learning the art of negotiation from his dad, was not going to let Almister get away with raising the price.

Almister sees promise in this young human, "Your price is a little low for some of these. Give me a fairer price." Almister with all three eyes on Russell, Michael and the others are nearly bystanders in this negotiation. Russell looks at J, J winks at him.

Russell replies, "I am sorry if we wasted your time and more so ours in coming here. I gave you a price, fair for both of us. We will leave now and go somewhere else and trade."

Michael waiting for Russell to motion for them to get up, J grins slightly knowing what is about to happen, Almister speaks up, "It is fair. You are smart young human. I like you. I will make plans for the goods to be ready when you need them."

Russell approached the desk and shook his center hand and thanked him. Michael was very proud of his son, for the work he put into the presentation and for negotiating the deal the way he did. The four of them exited Almister's office happy that their mission was a success. Rebecca and J were likewise very proud of Russell, now they too have a spring in their step.

Russell asked his dad, "Can we look around the city a bit? It truly is a sight for the eyes."

Michael could not say no to his son after that negotiation, smiling he replied, "Let's check to see if they have a pub in the area. Drinks on me."

The four of them exit the commerce building walking slowly to a nearby pub, entering they notice a variety of species that probably belong to the other ships they saw when they landed. They sit themselves at the bar, a young female Ternian came over with her dark green eyes and green complexion, leans into the bar exposing her ample cleavage, "What can I get you four?"

Russell unfamiliar with what they have on tap, "Four of the house specials." Having no idea what that was. The Ternian turned around to show her small waist and exposed back. Russell looked over at his father with a wow expression. Michael simply gave him a down boy type of look while Rebecca was keeping J in check.

The Ternian came back with four drinks in a spherical glass about eight inches round, the drinks were orange and steaming on its surface with a few bubbles making their way to the top. Russell looks at the drinks and then her, "What are the drinks called?" the young Ternian leans over pushing her cleavage as far out as they could go and whispers in Russells ear. Russell blushes a near perfect red. Rebecca asked, "well, what's the drink called?" Russell stumbled and muttered unintelligible words, obviously the young lady wanted more than a tip. Rebecca, J and Michael laughed at his inability to speak. They all raise their glasses for a toast of a mission well done and take a sip. Every one of their faces smiled as they finished their first sip, Rebecca, "This is pretty darn good!" Smiling and taking a bigger drink.

All four sat at the bar while the flirtatious Ternian brought drink after drink until Michael noticed they were drunk. Paying the bill he looked at J and motioned to help get these two back to the ship. J helped Becca putting her arm around his shoulders and his around her waist. Michael doing the same for his son. Michael thinking what to tell Kathy when they get back to the ship.

On the way back to the ship Russell kept slurring out how pretty Bontha is and Rebecca was slurring how pretty J was. This was quite the sight as both J and Michael assisted these two back to the ship. Michael was thinking that the drink had some truth serum in it.

Upon arriving back at the ship, Kathy noticed the two were assisting her children as if they were injured, she rushed down to the hatch to meet them. "What happened? Are they injured?" She asked in urgency with Alala right behind her. Both women looked worried. Michael smiled and at the same time sheepishly admitted, "No! They are not hurt, their injury will wear off in the morning and manifest itself with a headache."

Kathy punches Michael in the arm, "You got our kids drunk!" Kathy took Rebecca away from J and Alala took Russell away from his father, taking them to their quarters.

Michael and J stood there with a stupid look on their faces knowing they were both in trouble but still a little too drunk to care. They will care in the morning, they were sure of that.

Russell in Alala's arms looked up at her in his stupor, "You are so pretty. You probably don't know this because I hide it so well, but I like you. I like you a lot." Alala smiled at him as she got him to his quarters, "I like you to Russell, a lot as well." Alala admits to him. She helps remove his clothes and lays him down to sleep, she looks down at the man and smiles, thinking, 'a lot' as she closes the door behind her.

Rebecca in her mother's arms was going on and on about J, how cute he is, how handsome he is, how strong he is and on and on and on. Kathy gets Rebecca to her room and puts her in her bed. Kathy is mad at her husband and amused by her daughter's ramblings. Michael will not get out of this one easily.

Chapter 22

Back to the Eaglefire

Morning came and the Phoenix was already on her way through space. Michael, J, Rebecca and Russell all woke up with migraines. They all made their way to the sickbay where Alala had already started preparing shots to eliminate their headaches, one by one they went to Alala and received the easy part of the medicine that had to be administered. Kathy had some medicine to give as well.

Michael makes his way up to the bridge where Kathy is there flying the Phoenix, he enters the bridge, Russell is already at his station along with Lizzy and Rebecca, everyone is silent. Kathy is focused on the view screen, no 'good morning', no 'how are you?', no nothing! Kathy ignores Michael as he takes his seat knowing he is in big trouble. In over thirty years of marriage, Michael and Kathy have what he considers a perfect marriage, the trick is really knowing when to shut up. Allow the other person to process their feelings and do not push buttons! Not easy for an Italian family. Michael analyzes the gauges pretending to do something, Kathy is still looking intently at the view screen and holding the wheel, "Status?" Michael sheepishly utters.

Kathy robotically responds, "We are in deep space, those are stars and planets are behind us."

'Oh boy! She is fuming.' Michael said to himself. Michael and Kathy hardly ever get mad at each other and never discuss differences in front of the kids, so in this case Michael needs to talk to her privately. The kids see the reaction and are keeping their head down to avoid collateral damage. Michael reaches to a few switches and flips them, Kathy seeing what he is doing, puts it on auto pilot. She gets up and Michael follows with his tail tucked neatly. He knows he deserves what is coming, he will take it and then plead his case.

Kathy walks straight to the strategy room, Michael upon entering close behind her, closes and locks the door. "I am so mad at you!" Kathy sternly states. "What we're you thinking?" Michael knowing that this was the time to shut up, she continues, "You are on a foreign planet, perhaps with hostile on it and you lose your senses! What we're you thinking? " Kathy looking at Michael while he sits up and stares at her hoping to lock eyes which she avoids. Kathy sits down a couple chairs away from him, "What we're you thinking?" She said again but in a softer tone.

Kathy sits there now locking eyes with a disappointed look. Michael leans forward and after the pot loses some of its boil he starts to speak in a soft tone, "I am sorry! You are right, the decision to have a drink of unknown potency on a foreign planet with bad guys possibly there possibly endangering our lives and perhaps disrupting the relationship we have just created was stupid."

The long running sentence brings a faint smirk to Kathy's face. Michael knows she needed to vent and she needed to know that he sees why she was mad. The long running sentence was a way for him to ease the tension just a bit which seemed to have worked.

"I wanted you to sleep outside last night, OUTSIDE!" Kathy said with a small crescendo.

Michael seeing that she is starting to cool down, "If I wasn't a little tipsy I would have put on a space suit and tethered myself to the ship. You could have reeled me in in the morning."

Kathy at that thought cracked a small smile imagining her husband tethered to the ship at full impulse power. "I would not have given you a suit." She said with a smirk.

Michael feeling the ice was thawing, "I am sorry. You should have seen our son though. Almister directed his attention to Russell after learning he prepared the portfolio and started negotiating with him. Russell picked up the ball and closed the deal. He was magnificent! We got so excited and I was so proud of him that I treated all of us to a drink at a pub. It was a real task drink, too tasty! "

Kathy seeing that Michael was genuine and he praised their son with a glowing pride, she too was proud of Russell and understood the celebration. "You are not out of the dog house so quickly." She squarely said.

Michael softening her look with a small smile, “It’s been awhile since I have been in the dog house, I will poke my head out every once in a while until you are less mad at me.”

Kathy smiled, “You frustrate me sometimes! If I didn’t know you so well I would make you move into that house for a week.” She relaxed her pose.

Michael reaching over to hold her hand, “You do know me well, you know I am sorry and that I love you and the children more than life itself. I have no clue on how I discovered the perfect wife for me, and I don’t deserve the love you show me. I am an obnoxious, sarcastic and at times belligerent individual. Why you put up with all that humbles me.”

Kathy looks at him and curls her fingers around his hand, “It is those qualities with you unselfish love that makes me love you even more.”

Michael leans over to kiss her, she gives him her cheek, “You will work up to the mouth after a while.” She said with a grin.

“let’s go back up to the bridge, the kids probably think you killed me by now.” Michael said with a grin.

Sitting back in their seats at the helm, Michael asked Lizzy, “Lizzy? Do we have the coordinates of the Eaglefire?”

Lizzy responds, “Yes captain.”

"Please calculate our next jump point to intercept." Michael ordered.

Lizzy: "Aye captain."

Russell: "Permission to head down to sickbay captain."

Michael with a concerned look, "Not feeling well?"

Russell quick to put his mind at ease, "No! I feel fine, just need to take care of an issue."

"Granted." As Michael glances at Kathy with a grin.

Russell enters the sickbay with Alala tending to a few loos instruments a king his way over to her, "Are you feeling ok?" Alala asked.

"Come over here and sit down please." Russell motioning and leading her to two chairs, he has a seat after she does. "Last night I wasn't myself. To be honest I can count on one hand how many times I have been drunk, I don't want you to think I do that often." He looks squarely in her beautiful hazel eyes.

Alala pulls her hair from her face and leans forward, both facing each other, "You don't have to apologize, Rebecca filled me in on what happened, you should be very proud of yourself on negotiating the trade deal, I know I am."

Russell smiled closing the gap a little more, "I said some things to you last night, and alcohol lowers ones guard and allows them to speak without inhibitions." Alala smiled at him, "I wanted to wait to tell you those things, until I deemed it proper in timing. I hope you aren't afraid of my feelings."

Alala grabs both of Russells hands and looks into his eyes, "No, you did not scare me with your feelings, I have known them from the start. What you perhaps didn't know is that I have the same feeling for you."

Russell closes the gap while looking deep into her eyes, Alala meets him half way as their lips touch, Russell releases her hands and cups her face as they enjoy a prolonged Tender kiss. Backing away Russell sees her eyes slowly open and her smile widens, "I want you to stay." He said in an undertone.

Alala smiled at him closing the gap, "I want to stay." She said softly as she leans forward and kisses him again.

Rebecca on the bridge seeing that her brother is tending to what she knows is his feeling for Alala, feels compelled to do the same with J, "Permission to leave the bridge captain."

Michael grinning from ear to ear, "Permission granted." Looking at Kathy who likewise is grinning, "Two at one time?" Kathy smiled back with a shrug of her shoulder and palms up, "Looks like it." She says with a small laugh.

Rebecca enters the galley where she finds J enjoying a cup of coffee, "May I?" As she points to the chair next to him.

“Of course.” J responds politely.

Rebecca shows a lot of discomfort, apologies do not come naturally to her. She is the tough warrior and tries to play that roll twenty four seven. She though in this c are is humbled by her lack of self-control last night, “I want to apologize for my behavior last night.” She states softly.

J leans forward with holding his cup with both hands, “You don’t have to apologize.”

“Oh! But I do. I don’t do that often in fact that was my first time getting drunk. I try to stay in control of my senses at all times. I don’t want you to think I do that regularly.” Rebecca said with great seriousness.

J showing a small smile as he knows what kind of woman she is, plus he can read her thoughts, “I realize that. You were a little free flowing with your words too last night as well.” His smile growing larger.

Rebecca a little flushed at the realization she may have said too much last night, “Shouldn’t have come as no surprise to you. I realize you can read my thoughts which I find annoying. Still, what I said although true, doesn’t mean we can speed things up.”

J smiles at her words, “I agree. You were moving too fast for me last night. I mean when you…”

“When I what?” Rebecca interrupted him.

Smiling knowing she doesn’t remember everything and that she is playing out several scenarios in her mind, “well, when you grabbed my face and kissed me.” Now he is just trying to get a rise out of her.

“I did no such thing!” Rebecca insists.

“Well, I liked it anyway.” J gets up, smiles and then winks at her before leaving the room.

Rebecca sat their fuming at the nerve, then paused to rethink last night. Frustrated at the lapse of memory and at the thought of kissing him while drunk just frustrated her.

Michael summons J to the bridge. J arrives as ordered, Michael swivels his chair around while Kathy stays with the controls, “J, we are on our way back to meet with your father. I need to fill him in on Hegel, the fact that we used the Yag as pawns to facilitate a peace. If you wish, you may rejoin your father and his fleets.”

Rebecca, at her station looked at J with a lonely look, J seeing Rebecca addresses the captain, “Sir, if it pleases you, I would like to ask my father to allow me to stay with the Phoenix.”

Michael grins, glancing at Rebecca who quickly looked down on her panel, looks back at J, “We will see what your father say, you are still under his command, but if he is agreeable then I would welcome you to stay.

Lizzy: “Almost at jump point captain.”

Michael looking at J, “Dismissed.” Swiveling around to the helm, “Zeeke!”

Zeeke responds immediately, "Aye captain!"

Michael: "Get ready to initiate warp drive."

Lizzy: "Ready captain."

Michael hitting the comm button, "Initiate The Warp Drive!"

The stars around the Phoenix distorted and then snapped back to its new constellation.

Lizzy: "captain, the Eaglefire is four hours out sir at full impulse."

Michael looking at Kathy, "Let's go fill Primus in on all that we have accomplished."

Kathy smiled, "And a surprise too."

Chapter 23

The Eaglefire

Primus is on the bridge of the Eaglefire monitoring his team and receiving updates as they come in. He has a natural commanding presence to his military. His communication officer approached him, “Sir!”

Prim8s stopped what he was doing and turned to the young corporal, “What is it?”

Corporal Hans at attention addresses the commander, “The Phoenix sir is approaching the carrier. Permission to dock sir?”

Primus smiled at the thought of seeing his son again, “Granted! Have them escorted up to my quarters upon landing.”

Corporal Hans, “Yes! Sir! It will be done.” He about faced and communicated the order for the Phoenix to dock.

Primus calls over his first officer Major Devin, “You have the bridge major. I have a matter that needs my attention.” At that Primus left the bridge on his way to his quarters to await the arrival of his son.

The Phoenix’ hatched opened to a double line of soldiers, left and right leading to the escort waiting for them. Michael, Longbow, Rebecca and J exit the Phoenix to a simultaneous solute by both sides of the aisle. The reception was for the welcoming of a lost soldier, J. J led the team to the end of the line, as they pass each soldier, the soldier would lower his hand and stand at a perfect attention, one by one as they walked the soldiers would return to attention until they got to the end where Sargent Major Barlow stood. J stopped in front of Barlow, Barlow gave a formal solute to J. Barlow then extended his hand to warmly welcome J back to the Eaglefire. "It is good to have you back sir." Barlow said.

J reciprocated his words, "It is good to be back and out of that crab cage I was in. Primus in his quarters?"

"Yes sir." Barlow answered, "I am too take you four there where he can welcome you home personally."

"Lead on Sargeant Major." J replied. Then the four of them followed Barlow through the belly of the carrier and up the Aero Lift to a long corridor, Barlow presses a button on the wall next to the door, the door opened and Barlow motioned to the four of them to enter then he left to his duties.

Primus' quarters was large with a forward view into space, the room was one of several with a work station area. This room was about six meters by five meters with comfortable seating and a wet bar. Primus was standing in the middle of the room with a drink in his hand, when J entered he set down his drink and greeted his son with a hand shake while using the other one to grab his right shoulder in an affectionate way. "It is good to see you son." Primus said with a smile. "You look good. They didn't hurt you did they?"

"For a strange species they treated us well. I am uninjured. "J set his mind as ease.

Primus then turned his attention to the crew of the Phoenix, "Thank you Michael for giving me back my son. I owe your crew a large debt." As he shook the hands of each of them. "Please sit down and tell me what's been going on out there." Rebecca sat down in a small sofa where J also took his seat, Longbow and Michael take their individual seats across from Primus. Primus notices the seat his son took with curiosity.

Michael actually eats a drink from Primus, "We have been busy. As you know, there were two other prisoners with your son, Shayan's. We delivered them safely to their planet and then we're off to Bontha, there things got dicey."

Primus interjected, "Yes! J told me about the sick war two princes were waging."

"YES!" Michael continued, "We fought two fronts that day, one in space and the one we fought on the ground as we gained entrance to the castle. We played the preferred card we were dealt, your coalition. We threatened the princes using the Yag as the means if they didn't comply to our demands immediately." Primus with a grin, still listening intently, Michael continues, "The other card we were going to play if necessary would be the death of one of them or even both. Fortunately for them they chose the first option. The terms were simple, withdraw all the means they have supplied the two worlds to wage war and begin the rebuilding of their worlds."

Primus sitting now with a grin, "Seems simple to me. How did the negotiations go on Bontha?"

Michael with an affirmative tone, "I could not have been more proud of my son Russell. He took the lead in negotiations and was able to contract with Bontha the needed materials for our world."

"Excellent!" Primus exclaimed. "I will send a fleet from the nearby sectors to the Hegel system on a regular schedule to assure those brats keep their promise."

"That is indeed welcomed." Michael continues, "We need that trade route to remain open for our freighters to have safe passage."

Primus looking at Rebecca and his son, knowing the answer that he is going to ask, "Rebecca."

Rebecca looked At Primus directly, "Yes sir."

Primus smiled, "No need to address me formally. Do you wish for J to stay and help the Phoenix in finishing it's mission?"

Rebecca knowing he can read her thoughts, answered with a small smile, "We will be entering our solar system where we have a price on our heads still. I foresee some fighting and battles before we get back to Earth. J will prove crucial in those situations."

Primus laughed out loud, "Yes, I suppose you will also need him for those situations too."

Michael grinning at the implication.

Primus looking at Michael, "Tell me what plans do you have to remove the Orion syndicate from your path?"

Michael leans back in his chair with all eyes upon him, "Have you ever known me to not have a plan?"

Primus smiled back, "No!"

"Exactly!" Michael spills his plan to the group.

Chapter 24

Orion

Paul Orion gets word that the Phoenix not only has secured one of what would be the most lucrative deals in interstellar history but is on his way back to the sector. Orion summons Stan Whittaker to his office.

Stan enters to Paul pacing in front of his desk, Paul in a frustrated manner, "You failed me once Stan, I will not allow that to happen twice. You have one more chance to rectify that failure!" raising his voice slightly, "The Phoenix is headed back home as we speak, we have one more shot at it, I will not accept failure this time."

Stan looks at his old friend, not seeing anything in him that he used to see. Paul is obsessed, not just for profits but profits at any cost including the life of good people. Stan, in a calm manner tries to reason with Paul, "We have known each other since we were freshman in MIT, I have stood by you and supported you in everything you have done and accomplished, but this. This is something I think you should reconsider Paul."

Paul seeing not the reasoning but his old friend turning away from him, walks behind his desk and slams his fist down on it, “YOU! You dare to defy me? I expect you of all people to support me!”

“Defy?” Stan repeated, “Paul? I am not a child, I am your long standing partner and friend. If we go to Mike and partner with him we can share in the profits…”

“NO!” Paul interrupts Stan, “I will not give him that satisfaction! NO! This deal will be mine and all others past it.”

Stan for the first time was watching a stranger in front of him, the Paul Orion he knew was gone. What he saw now was a tyrant not a business man. Stan looked at the anger in Paul’s face, with great disappointment he said to the shell of his old friend, “I will not help you in this.”

“You are FIRED! Get out of here! NOW!” Orion yelled.

Stan holding a good percentage of the shares of this company did not get phased at the fact Paul fired him, he simply stated before turning and exiting the door, “What happened to my friend? What did you do to him?” Turning and leaving Paul in a rage in his office.

Paul Orion angrily hits his comm button and summons his chief of security before sitting down behind his desk. ‘The nerve of Stan to question me!’ He thought. His chief of security Gianni Carzoli enters the room, she is a determined woman with great ambitions, Italian with brown eyes and black hair with an athletic build standing at five foot ten, "Yes sir! You called for me." She said with loyalty in her voice.

Paul a little more relaxed now and seeing he has someone in front of him that will not question his commands, "Carzoli! I need you to arrange a welcoming committee for the Phoenix. I need that ship!"

Carzoli understands the request, "The crew?"

Paul with fire in his eyes, "Eliminate them. All of them."

Carzoli without emotion, "I will see to it myself sir."

Paul with a grin, "Dismissed!" At that Carzoli left his office to make arrangements for the crew of the Phoenix to die and recover the ship.

Stan headed to his office to grab a few things before exiting Orion Tower, thinking about what he could do to thwart Paul's plan to intercept the Phoenix. He gets into his Tesla roadster SRT and touches the screen to call Alex Treas, another member of the board of trustees for the syndicate and a trusted ally. "Alex, we need to talk in a secured location." Stan said with urgency.

Alex hearing the tone of his voice, "Come to my office."

Stan arrived at the Treas Center and made his way over to Alex' office. "What is this all about Stan?" Alex asked.

Stan taking a seat in front of his desk with all seriousness, "It's Paul. He has lost his ability to head the syndicate."

Alex in a not so surprised way, "What has happened?"

Stan explained the meeting he just came from in detail and what the Phoenix has been doing.

Alex asked, "What do you propose?"

Stan: "I want to contact the Phoenix and talk to Mike about teaming up. We have the resources to accomplish an interstellar trade deal, we have the ships and the crews, and he has the warp drive technology." Leaning forward with intent, "Think about it Alex. If we partner with him with our fleets we will make billions upon billions."

Alex is sitting back in his chair soaking this in and contemplating how they can do this, "What we are talking about is a hostile takeover and removing Paul from his position." Hand to chin, Alex continues, "We need a couple more board members on our side and Mike needs to agree. Mike needs to actively start purchasing shares in large quantities to get a controlling interest in the company. With the support you and I can solicit, we can do this."

Stan smiles, "I will contact the Phoenix and start the ball rolling."

Alex: “Excellent! Contact me when you have his agreement.”

Chapter 25

The Last Stand

Rebecca takes an incoming communication, "Captain! I have an inbound communication on a secured channel for you."

Kathy looks at Michael inquisitively, "Patch it through to my comm." Michael replied. In his ear is an ear bud he uses for communication. Kathy will just hear Michael speak. "This is the captain of the Phoenix."

Kathy seeing the surprised look on her husband's face just makes her more curious. Michael responding to the caller and the crew hearing nothing but the captains words he ends the transmission. Michael has a curious grin, looking over to Kathy. "That was Stan Whittaker, he wants to initiate a hostile takeover of Orion and he needs me to help him."

"I didn't hear you say no to him." Kathy commented.

Michael continues, "On the contrary, I said yes. It was my plan all along to take over that company, even now I have had a shell company buying up every share they could of Orion. What I didn't plan on was Whittaker. This will be a lot easier now with his help." Michael touches his chin with a concentrated look.

Kathy "What's the bad news?"

Michael looking at the view screen,"Stan informed me of a plan to intercept us when we enter the solar system."

Rebecca, "Did he give you any details of the plan?"

"Nope." Michael sat there thinking, "We knew Orion was going to try something, now it's just confirmed. When we come out of warp we will go on yellow alert as we journey back to Earth. We will be ready for whatever he will throw at us." Michael swiveling in his chair, "Lizzy, please calculate our next jump point as close to home as possible.

"Aye, captain." Lizzy quickly responded and started with her calculations.

Michael looked at Rebecca, "I need to meet with all the crew in the strategy room right away. Lizzy you stay here and finish that math problem."

Everyone including Zeeke assembled in the strategy room. Michael addresses the room, "We need to meet to discuss the upcoming battle when we enter our solar system." Michael turning to Rebecca, "Rebecca, fill us in on the different bases Orion has. He may use one or more of them to launch his offensive."

Rebecca gets up from her seat and makes her way to the rooms forward view screen, she pressed a button and the Earths solar system was visible. "Orion has several bases both in planet and off planet that he could launch an offensive." Pressing a button, the screen zooms in on Neptune, "The Neptune base will be the first we pass, although it is mostly built for mining, it has a contingency of two squadrons of fighters. These fighters look like this." Pressing another button, "The semi-circle has a pilot forward and the thrusters are on the flat side. The weapons are charged by running along the perimeter and discharging forward above the cockpit. These are equipped with energy weapons with a range of five thousand meters. These ships are agile and can match the maneuverability of the Phoenix." Rebecca pressing a button again, "Orion has his main base on Triton, Jupiter's largest moon. Here the Orion Syndicate has fourteen squadrons of three distinct designs. One I have just detailed, another is a five point star design, these too have a single pilot cockpit located at the axis point for the arms which all are equipped with impulse rays. The five rays are like being hit with an earthquake. Our shield are tough, but with a fleet of these we won't last long. The third ship is a "U" design, two pilots fly this ship one at the end of each arm, the main weapon is located on the curvature behind the pilot. This ship fires projectile weapons with a tracking system and proximity detonation."

J taking all this in, "Since I am new to the Phoenix, what ordinances do we have to neutralize these weapons?"

Rebecca grins at J, "We are well equipped in our weapons array. The Phoenix has enhanced weaponry. We have been able to modify the reach of our weapons by some one hundred and fifty percent. Our reach is longer than theirs. Our shields have been modified to resist all three of these weapons. The

Phoenix hull is reinforced in such a way that will last as long as our shield if not a little longer. The trick is engaging squadrons of ships, although we can outlast them and out range them the sheer number of them will be able to weaken The Phoenix or even worse."

Michael stands up, "I don't think they would destroy the Phoenix since what they want is on her."

"True!" Rebecca replies, "Crippling her is their target and then boarding us to kill us afterwards. We need a strategy to combat what we are sure will be Orion's last stand."

Zeeke gets up from his seat, "If I may." Makes his way to the front of the room, Rebecca goes to her seat, "I have an idea that may increase our odds. I have been fine tuning a new design of shielding. Right now we have used a Metaphasic shield and has worked quite well, but it has its limits. I have designed what I call a Deflective Shield. Most fighters are equipped with an energy based weapon." Everyone's attention is fixed on every word coming from Zeekes mouth, "An energy beam, whether it is an impulse or other forms is still just concentrated energy. The new shielding will cause the beam to deflect off of it like a laser bounces off a mirror."

Michael with great interest, "Will the ship feel anything?"

Zeeke smiled at the question, "it's not that good, and energy weapons still will give us a jolt. The shear impact to the shields will be felt but the weapon itself will be deflected. The interesting thing is, because of the shield the deflected weapon will either head into space or hit something." He had a great big smile.

Longbow, "Well, that takes care of two squadrons, what about those bloody other ships with Missiles"

Zeeke now has a serious look, "That is a problem, the new deflector shield only works on energy weapons, our current shield will still remain available but projectile weapons go right through it."

Rebecca chimes in, "We will have to man the missile array turret and intercept them before they hit us."

Zeeke goes to the view screen, "I have not forgotten about those. I have modified our current missiles to have a larger area of detonation of eight hundred meters each. With a spread of twenty degrees we can create a wall with the AOE that will detonate the incoming ordinance."

J enters the discussion, "Surely some will get through the concussion wall we lay out."

"Indeed!" Zeeke responding to the statement, "With several ships firing at us with an ordinance that has been programmed to our ships signature, I have created a type of flack we can release with our same signature that the missiles will follow and hit. Our strategy might have in focus those ships with projectile ordinance and how to defeat them."

Michael has been taking all this in as Zeeke sits down the room is quietly contemplating the information and trying to develop a plan, Michael heads to the front, "I think I have a plan to defeat this ambush. Zeeke, thank you, you're a genius! " Zeeke wonders what he has up his sleeve, Michael continues, "In order for my plan to work we need everyone in specific locations, Zeeke, you monitor shielding and have our metaphasic shielding available at a moments notice. Longbow, you will be in the turret laying out that concussion wall and intercepting that ordinance coming our way. Rebecca, you will be at the weapons station and J, you will be in control of the decoy flack. Lizzy, you will monitor all incoming. Russell and Alala, you two will be on the bridge to attend to any injured if we have any. Do you all know your assignments?" They all nodded in agreement, "Any questions?"

They all want to ask the same question, what is his plan? J is the only one in the room that knows other than Michael and J is smiling. Rebecca sees his smile and knows she can get it from J later.

Michael then says, "Well what are we waiting for? Lizzy get us to our jump site and all of us get ready for this battle."

They all rose and headed to their stations, Longbow topside level to the turret with can launch twelve missiles simultaneously on a turret that rotates three hundred and sixty degrees. Alala heads to sick bay to put together a medical bag for immediate treatment if needed.

Meanwhile on earth, Paul Orion sits at his desk monitoring the plans to intercept the Phoenix. He has given Carzoli all resource he has to accomplish this. Orion looks down at his desk at the inlaid monitor and sees an urgent memo of what Stan is trying to develop, 'That rat! He won't get away with this!' thinking as he reads the report from his corporate spies. 'The only way that will work is if he fails, and this will not fail!' convincing himself. This truly is Orions last stand.

Typing away on his key oars he sends a message to Carzoli. Carzoli relieves the transmission as she is just arriving on Triton at the fighter base. She types back that all things are about set in place and the fighters will be ready.

Carzoli arrives at the base in the corporate ship and upon landing she meets the bases commanding officer Jessica Martinez, an ambitious woman as well in her early thirties, brown hair and brown eyes, she too athletically built standing about five foot nine. Carzoli looks directly at her, "You received my communication, is everything ready"

Martinez, "I have three squadrons ready to launch at a moment's notice."

Carzoli without a stone cold look, "I am going to lead these pilots, I will need one of the star fire ships"

Martinez did not expect her to be in the fight, without hesitation, "Yes ma'am! One will be arranged."

The two of them walked to the hanger bay to prepare for the assault.

The Phoenix is at the jump location, Michael gives the order, "Zeeke, engage the warp drive!" Looking over to Kathy, "let's go have some fun." Smiling at her. The Phoenix engages her warp drive as the stars cape around them pulls and stretches before snapping back on the ship the familiar sight of their home star field sky is in front of them. The jump landed them between the planets Neptune and Uranus, "Yellow alert!" Michael orders.

The Phoenix engages her impulse engines at full thrust and the ship accelerates through open space, everyone's senses are buzzing looking at their screens and Lizzy trying to pick up anything on long range scanners. Michael conveys their location, "Passing Neptune, get ready Lizzy to see something." Nothing shows up on the screen for about an hour as they come into view of Jupiter.

"Captain I have a squadron coming up on our six one hundred Thousand kilometers, I Have Three SQUADRONS Just Launched From Triton. Each squadron has six ships. Intercept in fifteen minutes, thirty one seconds." Lizzy calls out.

"zeeke, Deflective Shield up! Red alert!" Michael calls out, "Longbow, keep your eyes peeled, you need to hold off that ordinance as I position the Phoenix. "

Longbow and Zeeke are heard over the speaker, "Aye, captain!" The crew are thinking 'position?' still not knowing all that is in their captains head. Kathy is monitoring the squadrons on the forward screen as Michael is calculating which ships are which ships. There are a total twenty four ships on two vectors to intercept the Phoenix, Michael is sure that the triton launch will break formation to flank him left and right as the get closer, ships should be at every quarter hour firing upon them, but which one will be the projectile ordinance fleet? He needed that information so he can calculate the Phoenix defense.

Lizzy calls out with urgency, "Captain! They are almost in firing range of the Phoenix."

"Rebecca and Longbow, get ready!" Michael commands, "Take your shot as soon as you get a lock on them."

Longbow sits in the turret pressing a few buttons and grabbing the yoke, he having the longest range in weapons, an alarm from his panel sounds, he looks forward and presses two buttons with each thumb on the yoke to release the first shots in this battle. Eight missiles launch from the Phoenix.

Carzoli is in the lead ship, "Incoming! Execute Orion Alpha." As she forcefully commands over the radio to the other squadrons. The three squadrons break left and right with one so the attack on all four sides of the Phoenix. The missiles arrive at the time of the squadrons execution of their strategy, with a larger than expected AOE, two of the star fire ships are destroyed. Carzoli yells on the comm, "Attack pattern Orion delta!"

Longbow yells, "Two splashed down!" his eyes looking at the squadrons on the screen separate aND try to out flank them.

Lizzy calls out to the captain, "Ultarian fighters are breaking to our three to flank us."

"Copy! " Michael calls out. He now knows where the projectiles are coming from, "J get the Flack ready, Longbow focus on our three for incoming!" Both men are at the ready focusing on their screens. Michael turns the Phoenix ninety degrees toward the Ultarian fleet slowing down to allow the other three squadrons to close the gap.

Lizzy calls out, "Captain! We are almost in range for their weapons." Lizzy looking down at her screen with wife eyes, "Incoming! Twelve of clock!"

Longbow releases twelve array missiles forward, as they fly toward their target he monitors the screen and the trajectory for intercept, at the press of a button all twelve explode in space causing a bright light to appear in a large distortion, the concussion of the blast is seen as a blur, the enemies missiles hit that wall and explodes in succession, all but one detonate because it was three seconds late in its launch.

“See it!” j yells! As the missile approaches he release the decoy Flack and the missile follows one to detonate safely away from the ship.

Michael is intently looking at the dots on the screen, “Lizzy! Tell me when we are in their energy weapons range.”

“In three, two, one!” She calls out.

Michael now pushes the Phoenix toward the forward ships as they launch another volley of missiles, the three other squadrons start their attack. From all sides yellow streaks approach from the ships three, six and nine o’clock positions while missiles come at twelve. Longbow releases another twelve while Rebecca fires the ships weapons at the squadrons, their shot hitting their marks, the array missiles stopping some of the inbound ordinance, too many weapons fired at once for the Phoenix to defend, then suddenly as the energy weapons hit the Deflective shields they bounce off of her at all angles hitting all that is around her. Missiles hit by the beams, enemy ships hit by the ricochet, explosions left, right, forward and to the rear are happening in quick succession.

Longbow aims at the inbound ships and takes advantage at the confusion, locking two missiles on each ship he releases the array missiles, hitting every ship in that squadron exploding them in space.

Carzoli watching the devastation happening in space, pushes her yoke forward with anger as she releases all her weapons at the Phoenix, bouncing off her shields she gets angrier and angrier.

Rebecca, watching this lone ship come at them in a desperate attempt zeroes in on the ship and releases the Phoenix last death blow to the ship, vaporizing it in the void of space.

Chapter 26

World Trade Federation of Ore

Paul Orion upon hearing the news slams his fist on his desk. With both hands on his desk he intently looks at his screen, hitting a few commands he gets up and heads out the door with a grin. He makes his way up to the roof top drone pad and gets in his Quadra copter and lifts off.

The Phoenix heads to earth, the team celebrates their victory with high fives and hugs. Kathy looks at Michael with a smile, “Nice work honey!”

“The ricochet was the keys, it was like we had dozens of weapons all firing at once, I just had to figure out where to put the ship.” He said with a silly grin. “Stay at yellow alert until we get to earth.”

Kathy smiled, “Aye, Aye captain!”

The Phoenix arrives at her home base on earth, at Michaels Mojave site, she is greeted by a host of mechanics and engineers. The facility is a large multi building complex with a main structure ten stories tall. With the welcoming committee was Stan Whittaker, the crew of the Phoenix exits the ship with Michael leading the way, engineers and mechanics enter as they exit, Michael walks up to Stan and shakes his hand. “I am glad to see you, we have a few things to discuss and finalize.” Stan said.

Michael: “I agree, let’s go to my office and talk about what we have to do to finish this.”

Alala and J have never been to earth, Rebecca takes J’s hand, “Earth has a lot more to offer than what you see here. I will make sure you get to see some of my favorite places.” J is enjoying the touch of her hand, earth? Who cares? he thinks.

Russell seeing his sister holding hands walks next to Alala, he touches her hand as she clasps it. “Your planet lacked vegetation.” She said looking around at the desert.

Russell laughs, “Well here it does. We are not far from the most amazing trees and natural wonders we have on the planet. We things settle down I will take you to Yosemite so you can see a little of what earth has.”

Michael and Stan enter his office, Michael inviting Stan to sit as he sits behind a large mahogany destination and a nice high back chair. “Have you noticed yet?” Michael asked.

Stan grinning, “Your shell company buying up Orion stocks? Yes.”

Michael with a surety in his voice, “The World Trade Federation of Ore has purchased a majority of Orion and I now am in position of control.”

Stan realizing this fact, "I have the board convinced that Paul was the wrong man to lead the company and that your company merging with ours gives everyone what they want. You get the armada of mining ships we have and you have the warp drive to enlarge the territory to any sector."

Michael smiles, "It does seem to be a perfect partnership. My company WTFO will assume the lead and orchestrating of off planet mining. I have a lead engineer that will head the teams, he likes to be called Panhead. Panhead will control the day to day operations of our ventures. As for the chair position at Orion...." Michael surveying Stan.

Stan seeing the look he is getting, "Me?" He asked in amazement.

"Yes!" Michael responds, "You know everything about that company and of late you have proved to me you have the companies interest above your own."

Stan is humbled by the trust Michael is giving him, especially since he ordered a plan to kill him just recently. "I am flattered and shocked that you would suggest me. I have to apologize for the incident outside the space station, I didn't want to do it."

"I know, I heard it in your voice and saw it in your eyes that day." Michael said with understanding, "I can't think of a better fit. Do we know where Paul is right now?"

Stan: "He is off grid right now. He has endless resources and some that I am not aware of."

Michael hand to chin, “He will resurface eventually, I am sure of it.” Michael leans forward to address Stan, “Right now, my team will refit a few ships with a warp drive and we need to get them to Bontha soon. The resources their will keep earth going indefinitely.”

With this merger, WTFO is able to mine and carry the trade resources from Bontha and other planets. Earth now has the elements to keep her population from grinding to a halt.

Epilogue

On the remote island of Niue in the south pacific, Paul Orion sits down with his head of his security on this top secret base. At this base Paul has a hanger bay deep within the mountains with launch tubes out the sheer cliffs above the crashing surf. "We will not be denied!" Paul exclaimed to Kevin Robinson. Robinson is a tall African with muscular arms and a bald head standing at six foot three.

"What is the plan boss?" Robinson asked.

Orion Stoudemire up and gestures to Robinson to follow, "Follow me." The two of them exit the office making their way to the hanger bays where teams of men are working. On an exposed gangway they stop and look over dozens and dozens of ships, "This is where we will launch our offensive in due time." Orion says with a grin that Robinson still questions as to what the plan is.

Stan Whittaker sits at Orions old desk atop of the Orion tower looking out the panoramic window to the lights of Los Angeles. He now has the power and position that his old friend enjoyed. Confidence and satisfaction is obvious in the way he purposed himself over the syndicate.

Michael and his family enjoy the time in their individual homes with their loved ones, Michael with Kathy, Rebecca with J and Russell with Alala. They are unaware of what Paul Orion is planning or what will happen soon in the vastness of space.

www.ingramcontent.com/pod-product-compliance
Lightning Source LLC
LaVergne TN
LVHW010556160826
845677LV00013B/3147